Praise for Fortune's Favor

This series just keeps getting better! I fell in love with the complex, sensual, cut-throat entrepôt that is the city of Beira on Menaechmi and with its equally complicated Guardian, then stayed up far too late, heart in my throat, to find out what would happen next. Lush, complicated—and thought-provoking—adventure. — Melissa Scott, legendary pioneering SFF author, winner of multiple genre awards

Graham's saga of *The Calpurnian Wars* is a perfect escape, everything I want when I pick up a space opera: characters to care about, a high-stakes plot, thrilling space battles, and a good admixture of politics and behind-the-scenes diplomacy. She also brings her own unique touch in the Hellenistic-influenced religions of the various worlds, founded as human colonies from a lost homeworld, and their relationships with the various gods and goddesses who still, through their human worshippers and avatars, exert an influence on the shape of events. With Fortune's Favor, I found myself drawn ever deeper into the developing greater story. // Every book in this series tells it own story, but taken together they're beginning to weave a larger pattern... // Meanwhile, the political intrigue and gripping ship to ship combat, influenced by naval rather than aerial warfare, continue to make for a great read. —K.V. Johansen, author of *Blackdog*

Fortune's Favor continues to develop and deepen the space opera world Graham introduced to us in *Sounding Dark* and *Warlady*, // a vivid canvas for Graham's penchant and skill for rich cultural details and complex societies that reminded me of Bronze Age Phoenician city states. Combine this with characters from the first two novels in the series, and new ones, and Graham shows how she's grown her world organically in this latest volume with a compelling story grounded in the very real and present desires and motivations of her creations. — Paul Weimer, SFF book reviewer and Hugo finalist

Familiar faces to the rescue as Graham gives us a new world to fall in love with and then immediately get incredibly concerned over. —E.K Johnston, #1 New York Times Bestselling Author

Praise for Warlady

Graham skillfully combines a murder mystery, political intrigue, and space combat in the intricate and thrilling second Calpurnian Wars space opera (after *Sounding Dark*). // Graham fashions an elaborate and fascinating world, complete with complex history, religion, and politics, without ever sacrificing the plot's forward momentum. This polished page-turner should hook any sci-fi fan. — *Publishers Weekly*

I love the rich, complicated world of the story, but it's the characters that really grabbed me: competent, clever, complex people, survivors who keep fighting for each other despite murder and invasion and all the rules of their culture. This one goes into the special group of books I keep to read and re-read. — Melissa Scott, legendary pioneering SFF author of more than thirty novels, winner of multiple genre awards

Thrilling battles in space, a murder mystery, a forbidden romance, and mature characters working to change their world, all set within another of Graham's fascinating cultures in her Nine Worlds, where far-future space opera meets spirituality with the flavour of classical antiquity—*Warlady* is a worthy sequel to *Sounding Dark*, and a story that leaves one feeling ultimately hopeful that maybe humans can after all find their way towards making a better future. — K.V. Johansen, author of the *Gods of the Caravan Road* epic fantasy series

Jo Graham's *Warlady* deftly moves the action in her Calpurnian Wars series to the planet of Morrigan, where politics, intrigue, the threat of war, and ancient secrets threaten not only the future of Sandrine, bodyguard to the titular Warlady, but the fate of the entire planet as well. Graham expertly weaves the personal with the political, making the fate and stakes of Sandrine's old relationship with the electromancer Jauffre as important and grounded for the reader as the fate of their entire world. — Paul Weimer, SFF book reviewer and Hugo finalist

Jo Graham combines two of my favourite things: a big galaxy and a personal story. With gently delivered backstory, deftly rising action, and a gorgeous re-romance, *Warlady* is for everyone who wants to build a better world. — E.K. Johnston, #1 New York Times Bestselling Author

PRAISE FOR SOUNDING DARK

Faith, luck, and grit propel this ambitious space opera from Graham (*Black Ships*). // Graham amps up the action, constructs a rich mythology of gods, cultures, and societies, and develops evocative characters that will make readers cheer. This pure sci-fi escape proves a fresh experience for fans who are tired of clichés. — *Publishers Weekly*

Sounding Dark is tremendously exciting space opera. // It's the sort of book you stay up far too late finishing, and then go back to re-read so that you can savor the details. The thing that's hard to express how well *Sounding Dark* blends solid technical SF // with deep myths. // Jo Graham makes both aspects utterly believable and equally crucial to the story. — Melissa Scott, legendary pioneering SFF author of more than thirty novels, winner of multiple genre award

Also by Jo Graham (selected works):

Black Ships

Stealing Fire

The Order of the Air
(series, Melissa Scott co-author)

The Calpurnian Wars:

Sounding Dark
Warlady
Fortune's Favor

A Blackened Mirror
(first in *Memoirs of the Borgia Sibyl* series)

FORTUNE'S FAVOR

Jo Graham

Candlemark & Gleam

For information, address
Athena Andreadis
Candlemark & Gleam LLC,
38 Rice Street #2, Cambridge, MA 02140
eloi@candlemarkandgleam.com

Library of Congress Cataloguing-in-Publication Data
In Progress

ISBNs: 978-1-952456-18-3 (paperback), 978-1-952456-19-0 (digital)

Cover art by Eleni Tsami
Book design and composition by Athena Andreadis

Editor: Athena Andreadis

Proofreader: Kelly Jennings

www.candlemarkandgleam.com

For my father,

who told me to go have some adventures.

PROLOGUE

Theo watched the Lesser Twin grow in the viewscreen, no more than a great golden ball, its brilliant light filtered by the cameras.

"Notify Menaechmi Control that we are inbound and our estimated arrival is seventy-three minutes," the captain said. She was a middle-aged woman with a no-nonsense manner, the golden honeybee badge of House Melian displayed on her blue shipsuit though this was a merchanter, not a warship. She looked at him and smiled. "Have you ever seen the approach before, Theo? It's impressive."

"No, Captain," Theo said politely. "I appreciate you letting me watch from the command center. I can't see anything from my cabin. There's only one screen."

The captain smiled indulgently. "Well, you're what? Twelve? If you've an interest, it's not too soon to learn how a ship works. Your sister Aurore is a fine pilot."

"She is," Theo said. Aurore was his favorite sister out of three, more than twice his age but always willing to join in whatever games he played or to introduce him to better ones. He did occasionally get tired of Aurore this and Aurore that, but it was hardly her fault that she impressed people or was fourteen years older.

The merchanter's three screens shifted, two showing views of the Lesser Twin, the third a starfield in which there was a small sphere, half-eclipsed. Home. Theo felt his heart leap. This had been his first trip alone, sent to Lono to stay with a factor of the House for his education. He'd learned a lot and some parts had been fun, but he hadn't quite realized how much he loved home until he was gone. It would be good to see his father and to play on beaches that were sandy and warm instead of rocky and cold.

"Captain, we are being hailed by another vessel," one of the crew said.

"Onscreen." The captain's manner was easy.

One of the displays changed, showing instead the brightly-lit interior of a ship, a man in close-up. He had tightly cropped hair and a scar on his chin prominent enough that Theo wondered why he hadn't had it erased. Only the collar of his shipsuit showed: Calpurnian red. "This is the *Liberty*. You will shut down your main engines immediately and prepare to receive a boarding party."

The captain's pleasant demeanor vanished in an instant. "On whose authority?"

"On the authority of the Calpurnian Senate, with myself as its representative." His mouth twisted a little, an expression of contempt. "I am Altissimus Cassian, duly rendered honors by that body."

The captain gestured to one of the crew beneath the level of the camera view on her, but her voice stayed even. "You are in the Menaechmi system. We are a merchant vessel with Menaechman registration inbound to our home port. Your authority does not allow you to detain us."

Theo felt a rush of fear. The Calpurnians had attacked Menaechman vessels before. But that wasn't supposed to happen anymore, not since his father and three other Guardians had given Altissimus Iulus a lot of currency. He sat down on his acceleration couch, sliding back and reaching for the straps.

"We see your registration, *Light Dancer*. What port are you inbound for?"

"We are inbound for Beira. We are the property of House Melian." Another gesture below camera level, and she swung the arm of her couch across her in the chair, her right hand moving on the board.

Theo bit his lip. The helmsman turned around and gave him a thumbs up. Theo pulled the shoulder straps across his body, fastening each at the opposite hip.

The man smiled. It wasn't a nice smile at all. "Shut down your main engines. We have business with your passengers." Theo's eyes widened. He was the only passenger of note.

The captain's voice was even. "I'm sorry, but we cannot allow that. You have no authority to detain Menaechman citizens in the Menaechmi system." Whatever the Calpurnian might have replied was silenced as the captain cut the comm. "Give me full power!" she said, and the screens tilted dizzily as she put the helm over hard, the Lesser Twin filling the screen, diving for the sun's gravity well like a sea bird fleeing a kestrel.

As the screens changed, Theo saw the other ship for the first time and sucked in a breath. It was a Calpurnian warship fully three times their size, black and sleek against the stars, enormous drive pod integrated so that it looked as slim and deadly as one of the massive toothfish that hunted in Menaechmi's seas.

"Captain, our structural integrity won't handle the coronasphere," one of the crew said.

"We're not going in. We're just going to try to lose them in the gravity well." The Lesser Twin grew on the center screen. "We'll put the Twin between us and then...."

"They're launching missiles!" another crew member shouted, their voice scaling up. Theo's hands tightened on the couch arms. He could see the flares of ignition on the screen with the rear view, the Calpurnian ship turning to follow as the missiles sped ahead of it.

"Send a distress to Menaechmi Control," the captain said. "And to Beira." Grimly, she angled the ship more steeply. "The structure will hold better against the coronasphere than it will against a pair of 500s." 500s. Theo swallowed hard. Those were the big missiles, ones that could punch through military armor. *Light Dancer* wasn't even armed.

"Missiles are closing, captain." Theo could see them on the screen. It didn't matter if the Calpurnian ship could catch them if they simply wanted to destroy them. Theo clenched his fists. He wasn't going to make a sound. "Impact in seven seconds." And then the missiles detonated astern, a rain of visible light as the ship shook. Alarms sounded.

"Captain, we have a breach in the stern hold!" one of the crew shouted, voice shaking with fear. "The compartment is sealed."

"The Calpurnians are hailing again," another said.

The captain dropped her eyes. "Put it on."

The man looked happy, Theo thought, like he was having fun. "The next missile won't be detonated short," he said. "Shut down your main engine and prepare to receive a boarding party. I will not warn you again."

She took a deep breath. She didn't look at Theo. "Yes, Altissimus. We are shutting down our engines. We protest this unlawful action and require you to inform House Melian."

Cassian's smile grew. "Don't worry. We'll inform House Melian."

Chapter One

The double suns of Full Day streamed down on the streets of Beira, their shared light dissolving all shadows. Beyond the seawall the whitecapped ocean broke in endless swells, a haze of evaporation hanging over it. No one was in sight. The heat was deadly. No one would venture from behind reflecting façades until the Lesser Twin set in five hours.

Caralys looked out through the mirrored glass of the sleek white trundle purring slowly through the port quarter. There was a low building with steps leading down to a door limned in blue light, now faded out in daylight brightness. "Stop here," she said. It was a live driver, not an automatic, and she pulled up as close to the building as possible. "Wait for me," Caralys said. "There's no traffic."

The driver nodded her assent, and Caralys braced herself as the side door opened up and out, making a small, shaded spot as though beneath a wing. The heat hit her like a physical blow. She swung her feet out, golden sandals better suited to indoors, but it was only a few steps. She hurried across the verge and down the steps, hearing the trundle closing up behind her.

Cool, dark—Caralys stopped just inside the door to get her bearings. The foyer was dark purple, a pair of chairs to one side, a standing desk to the other, all dimly lit by gold sconces. The curtains were drawn back across the inner entrance. An officious disson came round the desk, clearly ready to run off the unwelcome, and Caralys lifted a hand covered in jeweled mesh. There was no badge upon it, but it hardly needed one. "I'm meeting someone," she said.

"Of course, Gaura." They stepped aside with a gesture that would have swept back the curtains had they not already been parted, a place with greater pretensions to exclusivity than it had. In reality, it was simply one of the nicer starport establishments.

Caralys passed into the first room. It was larger than it first appeared, islands of tables separated by lush greenery, lit almost entirely by the aquariums that lined the walls and provided privacy between groups of tables. Most of the tables were empty. It was Full Day before a high holy day. Even though the holiday hadn't officially started yet, people had already begun their mourning. It wasn't seemly to be in a bar.

In the back, half behind a pruned bank of trees, there were two xalepiae at a table. And that was her party. Caralys made her way toward them, unhurried.

They lifted their heads as she approached. One was short and slight, wearing an ordinary brown shipsuit that didn't disguise her Menaechman origin, while the other was clearly a stranger, a dark-haired woman in a black, sleeveless top that showed tattoos on each shoulder, a star on one and an accretion disk on the other. The Menaechman stood up from her plush blue armchair as Caralys approached.

"Captain Ravit," Caralys said. "As always, a pleasure."

"Gaura Caralys," Jamila Ravit said with a deep nod, "the same. Allow me to introduce my associate. This is Bister. It's at her request that I've asked you to meet with us."

"I am delighted," Caralys said politely.

Jamila Ravit gestured to the attendant. "Beautiful Poison for us all. In ice."

"I appreciate you taking the time to see me," Bister said. Her face was weathered, though her voice and arms showed her to be not much more than fifty. "I represent…"

"After our drinks have come," Jamila said, taking her seat again as Caralys slid into the third plush chair, the one on the outside of the table. The wall behind was an aquarium, dimly blue-lit, with rocks and the waving fronds of sea plants. An octopus curled among the rocks, a tentacle or two lazily sampling the current.

"Your pardon," Bister said. "I am not Menaechman, so I hope you will forgive me if I don't know all the conventions."

"Of course," Caralys said. "And I am always pleased to meet a friend of Captain Ravit's. She has long been known to us." Caralys folded her hands; the gold mesh covering the backs of them attached to rings on each finger set with manufactured rubies, square cut and large, which then fastened to bracelets on each wrist. As she folded her hands, she discreetly touched the stud on the bottom of her right bracelet that activated the recording device.

Bister glanced at her hands appreciatively, or perhaps at the rubies, calculating their resale value. "Are you an Adept?"

Jamila shifted in her seat, but Caralys laughed. "Lord's Skirts, no! Offworlders think Adepts grow on trees, which they don't even on Menaechmi. I am simply a gaura in service to a single House. Captain Ravit has handled delicate trades for us before, and so I am here to listen to what she has to say. Which I presume is what you have to say."

"Just so," Jamila said. "And I appreciate your time." She gave Bister a warning look, a hint the other woman took immediately.

"I take no offense," Caralys said as the attendant approached with the drinks. "On Menaechmi sex is public and currency is private."

Wordlessly, the attendant presented three cold holders, each containing a cup made of ice. Into them he poured a stream of spirits and citrus syrup, setting them together at the center of the table. "Leave the pitcher," Jamila said, and he nodded and backed away.

Bister reached for the nearest cup, and Caralys followed. "That's a good punch," Bister said as she tasted it. "What is it?"

"Lime and kumquat," Caralys said. "And fermented succulent nectar." She took a sip. "And this is well made." The ice cup melted on the rim at the touch of her lips, but the cooler it sat in would keep it intact until they finished. "And now we will talk business if you like."

Bister glanced at Jamila, then directed her gaze to Caralys. "I represent Inanna," she said. "We've traded with Menaechmi before often enough in spite of the Isolation. But now we've warred with Calpurnia and made common cause with Eresh. We need a more robust bargain."

"And what would that bargain entail?" Caralys asked.

"We need official recognition from one of the member states of the original Alliance that imposed the Isolation. We need one of the signatories to the punitive bond to declare it is no longer valid and that Inanna is self-governing." Bister's eyes met hers squarely.

"You ask a great deal," Caralys said. She took another sip. "You do know that what you ask may not be possible?"

Bister spread her hands. "Go on."

"Firstly, Menaechmi has no planetary government. The Cities of the Coast are like jewels on a thread, seven sisters along the continental edge between the desert and the sea, each ruled by a Guardian. Sometimes we cooperate and sometimes we fight. Six million people live in Beira or its hinterlands, but we speak for no other City than our own. Beira's Guardian has no authority to treat for Menaechmi."

Bister lifted her cup with both hands, looking over the rim. "I've heard that Beira's Guardian can often move events in the direction he desires. Isn't he the Husband of the Golden Lady?"

"That is true," Caralys said, tilting her wrist to put Bister in a better camera angle. "But that power must be used sparingly. Which brings me to my second point. We do not have a fleet.

When the Altissimi park warships in orbit and politely request our cooperation, we have little choice. While we greatly appreciate your removal of Altissima Gnea, her death does not entirely solve our problems."

Bister nodded, acknowledging the compliment. "But now Altissimus Iulus is also dead and the Warlady of Morrigan has defeated the Calpurnian fleet."

"The Warlady of Morrigan has run their Navy out of Morriganian space, and the current Altissimi would be foolish to try Morrigan again. But as I said, that does not solve our problem. Various factions contend for Calpurnia. Even weakened, any of them have more starships than we do."

"Forgive me, but why don't you build some?" Bister gestured around the lovely room. "You have money. You have tech. Why don't you build a fleet?"

"If any City should attempt such a thing, the others would unite against it." Caralys shrugged. "It would be presumed that it was a weapon to use against our neighbors. If Beira began building warships, we would be attacked by the other Cities within a Day."

"So instead you remain at the mercy of Calpurnia when you don't have to be," Bister said.

"Calpurnia is distant, and so far their demands have been bearable," Caralys said. "While our neighbors are close and jealous." She took a sip of her Beautiful Poison. "To formally recognize Inanna would invite Calpurnian repercussions."

"Now less than before," Bister said.

"That is true," Caralys said. "None of the Altissimi are as strong as Gnea or Iulus, and many ships were lost at Morrigan."

"And Eresh," Jamila Ravit said. "I took one myself and put a prize crew on her."

"A formidable achievement," Caralys said, though she imagined it must have been one of the smaller ships. Still, there was a rising tide here that could not be ignored. "I will discuss your request in certain circles." She looked at Bister. "What do you offer, theoretically, in exchange for recognition of Inanna's independence?"

"Our friendship and open trade," Bister said.

Caralys tilted her wrist just a little. "Forgive me, but you also have no fleet, and we do not need foodstuffs from offworld as Eresh does. What do you have that we need?"

Bister didn't flinch from her gaze. "Once we were mighty."

"But you are not anymore," Caralys said quietly. "If this were in the days of the Alliance when Inanna was a great power, it would look different. But you are a low-tech agricultural world with a small population. I do not dispute that one day you will be powerful again. But in this day, we live with what is. We have no cause to love the Isolation. I doubt most Menaechman even care. It could be renounced without looking back. But what does matter is that we cannot declare ourselves the enemy of Calpurnia."

"Rather than a client state."

"If you like," Caralys said. "If Inanna reenters the spheres of the great powers, you will learn that being a client state is better than being a smoking ruin. We learned from your fate, did we not? Would any world be so stupid as to invite war and retribution?"

Bister let out a long breath. "No, of course not. No reasonable Guardian would wish the Isolation on his people. I've heard your Guardian is reasonable."

"If you had a proposal that were mutually beneficial," Caralys said, "I am certain the Guardian would hear it. And I am sure he will follow your progress with great interest."

"You sound certain of that," Bister said. "Is it possible to reach him?"

"I believe so," Caralys said. "And there may be some intermediate steps that can be taken toward friendship that stop short of the full recognition you ask that may be beneficial to Inanna. I will contact you if I have ideas on that. And do not hesitate to communicate with me again if you have further matters of interest." Caralys stood up, putting her cup on the table. "Captain Ravit, a pleasure as always. Bister, I was pleased to meet you."

"And I you," Bister said as they both got to their feet.

"Until we meet again," Jamila said formally.

Bister watched Caralys walk away, scarlet dress and chestnut hair bound in a golden caul that matched the mesh on her hands. "That was clear enough," Bister said. "Come back when you've got something worth trading."

"Still," Jamila said, taking a sip of her drink, "she's the best contact I have. You wanted highly placed. That's my best shot."

"A prostitute?"

Jamila winced. "A gaura. It's a different thing. A gaura is employed by one House, sometimes for decades at a time. She's not for sale."

"I wasn't judging," Bister said mildly. "There are lots of ways to make a living in the big world. Plenty of people find it expedient to make themselves likeable to someone able to support them."

"On Menaechmi we have rules about that," Jamila said. "Who can contract under what circumstances, what the rights of all parties are, what obligations are required. Even a pick-up in the starport requires ticking the disclaimers on their handheld to say that you've agreed to the terms of the contract." Jamila drained her drink. "That's true regardless of everyone's genders. I've always thought it odd you only have three instead of five."

"It's a big world," Bister said. "Are gauras all…" She searched for the word. "Elegant? Feminine?"

"Five genders instead of three," Jamila said again. "She's hapalia, but gauras can be any gender."

"Do you really think she can reach somebody's ear?"

"She's had some very interesting jobs for me in the past," Jamila said. "It's amazing how someone might want to travel to Calpurnia and not go through customs on the way in. You'd have no way to know they were even there."

"You've smuggled people onto Calpurnia?" Bister asked.

"And out."

"That's a lot harder than goods," she said.

"Tell me about it." Jamila pursed her lips. "And it pays commensurately."

That was Jamila, always about the bottom line. "Who did you smuggle?"

"Presumably some of the House's agents. Nondescript people with undefined business. Somebody keeps a close watch on what goes on in the Calpurnian Senate. But I couldn't tell you who the principal is. They like to keep it that way."

"If you don't know, you can't say," Bister said.

"Just so."

Bister shook her head. "I'm not seeing an in. Maybe I should have gone with Perisad to Morrigan first."

"And what does Inanna have to offer Morrigan?" Jamila asked. "They don't need shiploads of bulk consumables either. Also," she paused, "no offense to Perisad, Morriganians are weird."

Bister took another sip of the punch. It was really good. She wondered what a kumquat was. "Maybe I'm thinking about this wrong," she mused. "When I ran pharma, this was the deal: I'd get a load of agricultural produce and fresh meat from the clans up to Eresh and then sell it on Eresh for hard currency to people with limited growing space and no grazing space on an airless moon. Then I'd take the hard currency to Morrigan with Perisad and hit the shops where pharma is cheap, and load up on analgesics, sterile bandages, anticoagulants, antihistamines, you name it. Pick up a few entertainment data chips for nearly nothing, batteries, and anything else the clans need. Then smuggle all that through Eresh to Inanna where it's practically priceless. Then start all over again trading it for agricultural products." She looked at Jamila. "There wasn't anything Inanna made that Morrigan wanted. But run it through a third party, and suddenly everybody's problems are solved."

"So who's the third party and what do they want?" Jamila asked. She looked intrigued at the thought of a profit.

"I don't know yet," Bister said. "But that's got to be the deal, doesn't it? Somebody's got something the Guardian needs. We get it for him, and Menaechmi gives us what we need. Galactic politics isn't any different from a smuggling run."

Jamila laughed. "Sure. It's that simple."

"It might be," Bister said. "I just need to figure out the angle." She drained the rest of her drink. "Jamila, what's a kumquat?"

The trundle pulled around the back of the building, passing through two electronic checkpoints. Heavy watertight doors opened and then closed behind her each time, as the trundle descended into a basement garage two levels below the street. Caralys stepped out into cool air, white concrete walls as thick as she was tall providing both security and comfort. She lifted her bejeweled left hand to her face. "Assistant, where is the Guardian?"

"The Guardian is in his salia," a crisp voice replied. "Four Guild members are present. Shall I put your call through?"

"No," Caralys said. "Just a discreet chime. Thank you." She went in through the metal doors to a narrow lobby carpeted in rich blue, the carpet thick enough that her thin-soled gold sandals sank into it. A single bench was built into the far wall. A concealed compartment swung open at a touch, showing a dozen pairs of shoes and various wraps and outerwear. She stopped, slipping on tall pattens in scarlet that added a handspan of height, and then added a translucent gold shawl. The interior cool was chilly on her bare shoulders and back. Then she ran her hand over the call plate and stepped into the lift. "Twelve," she said briskly.

The inside of the lift was paneled in precious burled wood, a faint cedar scent clinging to it. When the doors opened, it was to a similarly opulent view. The entire wall to the right was a single panel of mirrored glass. Beyond it, Beira stretched up to the mountain's feet, the volcano like a sleeping beast beneath a blanket of green. One tiny puff of white showed at the summit. "The Old Man is snoring," as the old people said. In the heat of Full Day, you could practically see the vegetation steaming. As soon as the Lesser Twin set, condensation would begin. The Greater Twin would not be far behind in its decline, eleven hours of Greater Day until twilight. Then the storms would roll in from the restless sea.

The rest of the room was muted in color, the better to emphasize the beauty without. A low table held a long rough stone planter of sprouting grain, a concession to the holiday. Discreet detectors flared as Caralys turned to her left and passed through the archway into the next room. The assistant looked up from their workstation, one hand pausing over the security button, then moving when they saw who it was.

"In his salia, you say?" Caralys asked.

"Yes, Gaura. Do you want me to send anything in?"

"That won't be necessary." Caralys gave them a smile. "What is on the schedule next?"

"Given the holiday, there are no further plans until the last hour of twilight," the assistant said. "I presume since the Guardian is not sleeping during the middle of the Full Day…." They let their voice trail off.

"You presume the Guardian must sleep at some time, yes. I will call for a meal if it is wanted." She patted the assistant on the shoulder as she passed, then paused a dozen feet down the hall, her tall pattens leaving impressions in the thick carpet. "Which Guild members?"

"Callista, Haro, Themistin, and Lesk."

Hardly favorites. "Thank you." Caralys continued down the

hall, running her hand over the entry plate and opening the door at the end, sweeping in with a smile.

Along the near wall stood a small shrine to the Golden Lady, graceful and masked, her foot on the prow of a starship and a cascade of treasure pouring from the pitcher she held. Three indigo couches were arranged in a semi-circle at the far side of the room, each with a little table beside it, facing the windows that looked to the sea. The city of Beira lay at their feet, and beyond the cerulean waters rolled ever onward, a few clouds gathering far out to sea. The tempered glass dimmed the Lesser Twin to a ball of gold even now descending to the waves, perhaps twenty degrees above the horizon. Its light caught on the skin of an incoming starship, boosters flaring to tilt it upright for its landing at the starport. Small, Caralys thought, but with a missile tube from the shape of it. That was interesting.

All eyes turned to her entry. Callista and Themistin occupied the two side couches, Lesk perching nervously on the foot of Themistin's. Haro stood by the window, his pale blush skirts of many layers of silk moving in the cool air blowing from the ceiling vent, his long chiffon coat open at the front with no shirt beneath it. Bare-chested was not a winsome look on him, Caralys thought. At a certain point in one's life one should either abandon it or spend a great deal of time in the gymnasium. The pectoral of pale amethysts he wore only emphasized his paunch. Themistin was also a heavy man, but his clothes gave him gravitas rather than making him look like ram dressed as lamb.

"And there is my dear Cara!" The Guardian Helios Melian reclined on the center couch, leaning on his left arm. His silks were one shade darker than the upholstery, a color that complimented his saturnine complexion and dark hair artfully streaked with white at the temples. The smile he gave her was genuine as he reached for her with his right hand, and Caralys came around the couch and dipped to kiss it, eyes cast politely down. When they flickered up, she saw the lines of stress around his smile.

"I am so glad to see you all," Caralys said, sliding in to sit beside him in the curve of his body, her back against him, rather a trick to do gracefully in the pattens. "I don't mean to interrupt your business."

"Nonsense, Cara. You are never an interruption. We have been discussing very boring things for quite some time." He spoke to her, but she saw Haro stiffen.

"Does this mean that you are prepared to take action in the matter of the water works, Guardian?" Haro asked.

"It means that I will carefully consider it," he replied.

"I should hope that you…" Callista began. She was the Guardian's own age, her hair pinned up beneath an elaborate headdress.

He waved it off. "I'll consider it. Business, business. Do none of you have any pleasures to go to?" He squeezed Caralys's waist. "And you are a vision. Is she not lovely, Callista?"

"Very fetching," Callista said dryly. "And I've said as much for several years. Now about the matter at hand…."

"We'll discuss it after the holiday. It's Full Day and late for a rest." The Guardian looked at Caralys like a besotted boy. "Surely it can wait until the Golden Lady has had her due."

Lesk caved in first. "Of course," he said. "Then I will take my leave of you, Guardian. And of you, Gaura." He got to his feet.

Of course the others had to as well. Part of the meeting could hardly remain after it was over. Caralys ushered them to the door, making pretty compliments to all and sundry and apologizing profusely for interrupting such important business. She thought that Themistin might be genuinely charmed rather than irritated.

When they were all out the door, she turned around. Helios was decanting a cup of wine for her from the standing urn along the wall, the pearls and gold on his fingers catching the sheen of the descending Twin through the window. "I thought they'd never leave." There was nothing light in his voice, his back stiff even as he bent to fill the chased silver cup.

Caralys kicked off the pattens and crossed the floor quickly. "My dear, what terrible thing has happened?"

He handed her the cup and then turned to refill his own. "There is a Calpurnian warship in orbit."

The silver was cool in her hand, but she didn't drink. She watched him decant a second cup. "Yes, that's a serious problem. Which faction?"

"Altissimi Cassian and Junia." Helios lifted the cup to his lips, but barely sipped. "The assassins themselves. The ones who killed Altissimus Iulus after his return from the disastrous military action against Morrigan. I gather from their presence with one warship between them that they're on the run from other factions."

"And so they want currency," Caralys said. She shook her head, stepping around the couch to sit facing the little table.

He joined her, sitting at the head of the couch, his shoulder almost touching hers. "They want currency. If that was all they wanted, I'd simply give it to them. But they demanded skilled merchant spacers to be culled from Menaechman ships and raw military recruits for the Calpurnian Navy, young people to enter their service." He turned the cup round in his hands, apparently examining the scene of revelry upon it. "I told Cassian that was impossible."

"Obviously it is," Caralys said. "You don't have the authority to simply seize young people from their families and send them to the Calpurnian Navy, no matter how desperate Cassian is for raw recruits! Or to press unwilling merchant spacers. That's not the kind of thing we've ever done. You're not an autarch with that kind of despotic power. There's no law that provides for that."

"Cassian responded that I'd better make some law." Helios's mouth set in a grim line. "Or he should have to become more persuasive."

She took a deep breath. "Or they'd attack Menaechman ships?"

"They already have." Helios met her eyes. "They have Theo."

Caralys felt a cold wave drop over her. "How?" she managed.

"His ship was inbound from Lono. The captain tried to flee by ducking close to the Lesser Twin, but they flushed them out with missiles. Theo was unhurt. Cassian presents to me his hopes that he remains that way." Helios's jaw clenched. "They will pay for this. If one hair on Theo's head is harmed, I will tear him apart like the entrails of the Bull."

"I know you will," Caralys said. It was moments like this that she was glad she was cold, glad of self-discipline and mental tricks that allowed emotions to be put in neat little boxes and shoved into storage for later. Helios was never cold. "What about Aurore?" she asked. Theo's oldest sister was no slack strategist.

"Aurore won't be back for at least four Days. This venture on Freya demanded her eyes, and I can't imagine it will go any faster than that." Helios put the cup down with a click on the marble surface of the little table.

Four Days, two hundred and fifty-six hours. No, Helios couldn't possibly stall Cassian that long. "And there's the high holiday," Caralys said. "Do you think they timed it this way on purpose?"

Helios snorted. "I doubt Cassian has any idea of our calendar or the significance of any particular day. Junia? Perhaps." He spread his hands. "It certainly increases the pressure, doesn't it? If word of this gets out, or that I am considering acquiescing to their demands...."

"You wouldn't." Caralys stared at him.

"Our young people against the entirety of Beira?" Helios got up, pacing over to the windows, the city at his feet in the light of the setting Twin. "Their missiles would kill tens of thousands if they fired on us from orbit. Perhaps hundreds of thousands. They could level much of the city with five missiles, and they probably carry twenty on a ship that size."

"They will say it is for Theo." She stood up.

"Of course they will." He didn't look at her. "I told Cassian I would negotiate." Caralys said nothing. "That it would take me time to fulfill his demands. What else would you have me do? Tell him to start shooting? Watch him torment Theo on camera? I need time. I need room to maneuver." Helios jerked his head sharply. "Delivering what he asks for is the last resort."

Caralys came to stand beside him, the cup in her left hand and her right arm around his waist. "Very well. Currency is easy."

"The amount he wants will very nearly empty the discretionary fund. But there's nothing to be done about that. And of course they want Calpurnian currency, but I can exchange for Calpurnian datasticks. There are enough of those in Beira." Helios shook his head. "No, the currency isn't the problem. The first is to get Theo off their ship safely. The second is to prevent them from using their missiles against us if we don't turn over the recruits. I can almost see how to solve the first but not the second." He held up one finger as if thinking, his profile against the endless sea and sky.

"So, how do we do the first?" she asked.

"The party that goes aboard to deliver the currency datachips frees Theo and takes him with them."

"Ah. Of course. So simple," she said.

"I said I could see how to do it, not that it would be easy." He tapped his hand against his lips.

Caralys took a sip of her wine. The cup rang against her bracelet. It reminded her of something. "Actually," she said slowly, "I have a useful asset. I met with a smuggler today who's gotten agents onto Calpurnia for me. She might be able to get someone on a Calpurnian ship. She had an associate who isn't Menaechman who struck me as capable." She disengaged her arm from his waist, lifting her right wrist and holding out the bracelet. "I'll show you." She pressed the replay, the tiny image projected on the white wall beside the window.

"Of course, my treasure." He watched thoughtfully as the entire conversation played out, Bister and Jamila Ravit discussing what it would take for recognition of Inanna.

"I said we couldn't anger Calpurnia, but under the circumstances—" Caralys said as the recording ended.

Helios spread his hands, the pearls on them catching the ruddy light of the Greater Twin. "If we steal Theo back and somehow prevent them from launching missiles, angering them is the least of our worries. As for the Isolation?" He snapped his fingers. "Frankly, who cares?"

"That's what I thought you'd say." Caralys smiled.

"There's no advantage to enforcing it. If there's an advantage to repudiating it, why not?" He tilted his head back, taking a deep breath. "You think this xalepia can get onto the Calpurnian ship and get Theo?"

"It's possible. But what then?"

"That is the next problem. What is to stop them from simply pounding us from orbit?"

Caralys paced halfway around the room, stopping in front of the shrine of the Golden Lady. "We lure them here? To celebrate the holiday or something?"

"And then kill them?" Helios stood behind her, one hand at her waist. "They'd have to be incredibly stupid or incredibly arrogant to do that. I expect you could get Cassian to lose his wits, my love, but Junia is made of sterner stuff. And if you recall, I will be very busy."

"I know. The rites require you."

"To say the least." There was a touch of irony in his voice. "I doubt the Golden Lady will excuse me. She will want her Husband."

"If Aurore were here...."

"We can't stall that long." Helios was silent for a moment. "Sabotage the missiles and destroy the ship?"

"If my contact can do it," Caralys said. "That's much more difficult than just getting Theo off. It's a warship. Its missiles surely aren't lying around where anyone can get to them."

"Hardly." He looked thoughtful. "I'd gladly deliver them to the rival Altissimi, but we have no idea where they are, and I suspect if we sent a ship to Cassandreia they'd want to know what we were doing. We'd need to capture them and hold them. Which brings us to the holy day again. It might be possible to get one of them as a counter-hostage."

Caralys put her head to the side, considering. "Do you think Junia would trade Theo for Cassian?"

"Possible but doubtful. More likely Junia would lob a missile at one of the other cities and demand his return. And Cassian certainly wouldn't trade Theo for her." He looked ruefully at the statue. "And that wouldn't do. The Golden Lady wouldn't like it." Caralys's eyebrows rose. It always disconcerted her just a little when he talked like that. "Why are the eyes of statues always empty?" he asked.

"Because they're stone," Caralys said.

"They should be sea-colored."

"I suppose." She leaned back against him. Theo was his favorite child, much as he loved all four of them. He was taking this hard. "Have you eaten?"

He shrugged. "Just wine with the Guild members."

"Then I will send for a meal," Caralys said, "and afterwards you should try to sleep. I'll reach out to my contact again and find out what she can do. It may be that she can at least get Theo away and deprive them of their bargaining chip. If she can get people off Calpurnia, perhaps she can get him off a Calpurnian warship."

"Perhaps so," he said, but didn't argue. Instead he carefully tipped a little of the wine in his cup into the bowl at the foot of the shrine. "Fortune's favor," he said.

Chapter Two

The tug released its hold as the Morriganian scoutship *Spider* settled into berth 122. "Systems are blue, Captain," Over-Lieutenant Paloma Arlan-Rea said, checking the screen on the arm of her couch. "We have a positive seal."

Not that a positive seal was critical here, Boral thought from the corner couch, the one that had been shoehorned into *Spider*'s tiny command center during the recent crisis. Menaechmi had a perfectly breathable atmosphere. It wasn't like an orbital station where a seal leak would depressurize the ship. It was the first time he'd been on a planet other than Morrigan. Would other air smell different even if it had approximately the same composition?

"All systems to standby," the Old Man said. He was twenty-seven, eight years older than Boral, but had a kind of world-weary charm that Boral hoped to emulate. There was a stir as everybody started locking down their boards and changing their couch positions at the same time. "Wait! Wait! Wait!" the Old Man said, overriding the noise. "Put me on shipwide and everybody be quiet for a minute."

Paloma switched it over. "You're on, Captain."

The Old Man shook his head. "All right, crew of *Spider*, listen up! Unless you are on Chain Watch, you are at liberty for forty-eight hours. Do not—and I repeat, do not—let me hear of any trouble. I do not want incidents. If you are in the second group to serve Chain Watch, I want to see you back here in twenty-three hours, sober, fed, and capable of standing watch! Is that clear?"

"Crystal clear, Captain," replied Kindy, the navigations officer.

"I expect everyone to behave in a way which will be a credit to the Fleet," the Old Man said. "If you are unclear about what may cause offense on Menaechmi, I suggest you read the cultural circular I sent yesterday. If you do not read it, ignorance is no excuse." Boral had read it. He'd read it five times. "There is also a list of things you may not bring back to the ship, including fermented consumables and people. If you are unsure what the difference is between those two things, please ask the watch officer and then report to medical." Boral supposed that was intended as dry humor. He had the firm intention of working on dry humor. It was practically essential to an action hero. "Now, go! Except for the Chain Watch, who may begin weeping." The Old Man cut the comm.

Kindy had already locked his board down. "Paloma, are you ready? Sparky?"

"I'm ready," Boral said. At first he'd bridled at the nickname, and then realized it was lovingly meant, for some value of loving.

The Old Man settled back in his seat. "Have fun, Paloma. I've got the first Chain Watch myself. See you in a bit."

"I'll be on time, Captain," Paloma said. She had the second Chain Watch. Presumably then the Old Man could have liberty. Paloma crept around the cramped couches, followed by Kindy and Boral. *Spider* was tiny as ships went and adding an extra couch to the command center for an electromancer had crowded everybody. Still, getting out of the last battle with a giant hole in the wall of the mess instead of being blown to pieces made everyone forgive a little crowding. Sparky was mega-positive.

Boral followed Kindy down the tiny corridor, patting his shipsuit pockets. Yes, there was his datacard with a small currency balance. He hadn't actually been paid yet—or at least he hadn't before the ship left Morrigan, but Master Castal-Edo had advanced him what had seemed like a lot of currency at the time. It was somewhat less after sixteen days shipboard. He needed more practice at games of skill, clearly. Maybe when they got back, if the Fleet hadn't figured out how to pay electromancers, Master Castal-Edo would advance him more. Surely he would if Boral asked nicely and explained all his expenses.

Red was waiting by the ventral hatch, the ramp extended into the port tube. She was a tall, angular woman a couple of years Boral's senior, engineer's hammers pinned to her collar. As always, she looked fantastic. "Everybody ready?" Red asked.

"Let's go!" Kindy said. "Let me tell you, worthies, the fun you can have on Menaechmi!"

"Is it a real party port?" Red asked.

"Let me just say that you don't have to pay for the peep show," Kindy said. He slapped Boral on the back. "We're going to give this young gentle an education!"

"For saving all our skins," Paloma said. "I told you I'd buy you a drink, Boral."

"I did too," Red said with a smile that made her freckles practically glow. Did freckles glow, Boral wondered. If not, how did she manage to practically illuminate the world? Well, so did the Captain, but differently. It was all very confusing.

"I owe you a drink too," Kindy said. "So that's three. Bar first!"

"Excellent plan," Paloma said. "Customs, then a tram. I know a good place."

Boral followed them through a checkpoint where a bored-looking person in some kind of uniform asked for their IDs and length of intended visit and out into a mezzanine over a glassed-in lobby full of trees. It was very loud and very busy.

"Now that's what I mean," Kindy said, nudging him.

A young man with three days growth of black beard and artfully disheveled hair was leaning against one of the planters, his tight black leather pants outlining every bulge, his black leather vest open in the front. He was chatting with a young woman, her hair pinned up with glittering combs, her green pantaloons and top so transparent that he could see the dark shadow of her nipples. She laughed, little bells on the fringe of her top ringing.

"Wow." Boral stopped. "I read that…"

"They have really different rules about modesty on Menaechmi," Paloma said. "We come from what's called a privacy culture, sociologically speaking."

"Which I'm sure they teach all about in officer's college," Red said. "In engineering we don't do the humanities like that."

"I appreciate the humanities," Boral said. The man was leaning in, showing the woman with the bells something on his handheld, his chest smooth beneath his black leather. "Lots of humanities."

"They have five genders instead of two," Paloma said. "There are hard women, soft women, doubles, soft men and hard men."

"Come again?" Boral said.

"Look, they put a lot of emphasis on appearance," Paloma said. "We've got two genders but what you look like doesn't have anything to do with what your genitals are."

"Nobody can see them anyway," Red said. "Unless you're close." She glanced at Boral and he felt himself blushing.

"It only matters when you're being a progenitor if you can genetically contribute a Y chromosome or not. Which has nothing to do with having sex or what genitals you have." Paloma shrugged. "They just do things differently. And some people elect to modify their bodies to have both sets of sexual characteristics. They're doubles. It's just a Menaechman thing."

"That wasn't in the cultural circular," Boral pointed out.

Kindy snorted. "That's because sex is private, Sparky. Well, to us. And the circular is a Fleet document. You think the Warlady passes around instructions about how to pick up someone on Menaechmi?"

"Probably not." Boral swallowed. He'd met the Warlady. He certainly wouldn't want to talk about sex with her.

"So what was in the circular?" Red asked. "I didn't read it."

"Um, don't try to borrow money?" Boral said. "Charging interest is illegal and there are predatory lenders who will try to lend tourists money but don't do it?"

Red looked at him sideways. "So how are people supposed to pay for things that they can't afford?"

"You can borrow against the value of something or get your House to fund something like starting a business," Boral said. "Or if it's like paying for professional training, people our age whose families can't afford it indenture themselves. So like if I wanted to be a medic and I was good enough, I'd get a life center to indenture me for seven years and I'd learn to be a medic and work for them while I learned. You live in a dorm and stuff like at an Academy. Lots of people learn professions by indenture, but it's competitive."

Kindy shrugged. "That's not that different. You have to compete to get into the Fleet and you have to promise five years' service."

"My mother borrowed currency to pay for my engineering school," Red said. "But she has to pay it back. That's where most of my pay goes."

"I wondered why you were always broke," Kindy said. "I thought you were just a lousy gambler."

"Very funny," Red said.

"Oh, and you can't share hotel rooms," Boral said. There was some strange stuff in that circular. "But I can't see why we would waste currency on a hotel room. We can stay on the ship for nothing."

"If you can't think of any reason you'd need a hotel room, I can't help you there, Sparky," Kindy said.

"Why can't you share hotel rooms?" Red asked. "So you won't pick someone up?"

"No, it's some weird thing about how it's not healthy and sanitary for more than one person to share a sleeping space. There's a big cultural taboo about 'co-sleeping'," Boral said. "Which is having more than one person in a room."

"There's four of us in our cabin," Red said. "And the only thing unhealthy about it is Kindy's socks."

"Only two in my cabin," Paloma said smugly. "I'm senior to you so we're only two to a cabin and no upper bunks."

"Well, it's apparently a big deal here," Boral said. "Sharing a room is super kinky or something. That's what the cultural circular says."

"So was there anything in that circular about anything fun?" Kindy asked.

"There's some kind of big cultural festival coming up," Boral said conscientiously. "The Death of the Bull and the Holy Wedding. It's one of the biggest holidays of the year. There's a parade and public rituals that are supposed to be something. Also lots of significant art is on display. I thought I might go." Everyone was looking at him. "You know. To see art."

"Suit yourself, Sparky," Kindy said. "I'm planning on seeing a lot of other things."

"I might come with you," Red said. "It sounds interesting." Boral felt himself blushing again.

"Well, I can't," Paloma said. "If it's not soon. I've got to be back and take the Chain Watch so the Captain can have liberty."

"I'll have to look and see exactly when it is," Boral said. "I'm completely confused between Menaechman days and ours. With two suns their calendar is a nightmare."

"Yeah, tomorrow is like next week or something," Kindy said. "But an hour is an hour. So it's easiest to just count hours."

"I've got a question," Red said to Paloma. "What if we run into Calpurnians in port? There was a warship in orbit. What if they have crew at liberty too?"

Paloma looked serious. "First of all, we're at peace now. The Warlady signed an armistice with them right after Altissimus Iulus was assassinated. So supposedly they'll stay out of our business and we'll stay out of theirs."

"Like that will happen," Kindy said. "Come on, Paloma. We've fought two wars with them in twelve years. It's going to come down to ass-kicking again."

"Maybe so, but not here," Paloma replied.

Boral felt he had to put something in. "The Warlady would kill us if we started something with the Calpurnian Navy. Also, we're a scoutship with a crew of thirty. That's a ship of the line with about six missile tubes to our single. If we were going to start another war with Calpurnia, this wouldn't be the way to do it."

"Sparky's got sense," Kindy said.

"I'm the one who'd have to try to stop six missiles at a time," Boral said. "And I can't do that. So let's not, all right?"

"One at a time was good enough for me," Paloma said with a lopsided smile.

"Yeah, let's not do that again," Red said. "How about we leave the Calpurnians alone, no matter what assholes they are?"

"They're probably not having liberty since they're still in orbit, or if they are, there are seven Cities of the Coast to choose from," Paloma said. "Our chances of running into Calpurnian Navy crew is tiny. So let's just go have fun and let them be."

"Got it," Boral said. He squared his shoulders. "So what's our first stop?"

"Dinner?" Paloma said. "And drinks? And then we can check out the scene. Just scrolling through, it looked like there were a whole bunch of specials and street parties with this Killing of the Bull thing. Look at this," she said, waving her handheld at them, "Bull's Blood cocktails two-for-one at the Hangar. No cover charge."

"Sounds good," Boral said. No cover charge would make his

paltry amount of currency go further. He wished there was a way to hit Master Castal-Edo up remotely. "We have a mission!"

The Greater Twin was finally setting. Bister wiped the sweat off her forehead with one work glove, stepping out from beneath *Naga*'s cargo ramp. She was wearing a sleeveless shirt, but she was still dripping in the heat which radiated up from the concrete tarmac where the armed merchanter was berthed. Jamila Ravit was offloading cargo. The entire crew and a few Menaechman day workers were getting everything off and onto metal pallets for delivery.

Bister was helping, of course. She hadn't paid for her passage, so she owed Jamila the work. It certainly wasn't the first time she'd handled cargo. She'd done a lot of odd jobs through the years, paying for her passage one way or another, before luck or the whim of the Lady of the Void had given her a purpose she'd never imagined, securing the freedom of her world from the punitive Isolation imposed generations ago. They needed trade and to get that they needed at least one of the original members of the Alliance to repudiate the treaty that had established it. It had seemed like Menaechmi—luxurious, fragile Menaechmi—was the most likely to do it; but as she looked off across the tarmac wavering in the heat, Bister wondered if this was a good idea. After all, Morrigan had just fought a war with Calpurnia. Maybe they had the better reason to repudiate the treaty, if only to annoy Calpurnia. Well, if this didn't work, she'd try Morrigan next. Her old smuggling buddy, Perisad, said he had some contacts there.

Jamila Ravit came around the end of the ramp, a datapad in her hand. "Hey Bister, I missed a ping from Caralys. She says she wants to talk to us about a job."

Bister frowned. There was a stir of breeze off the sea, and its coolness sent a chill down her back. "We just saw her. What's with that?"

"Probably needed to talk with her principal, whoever that is. She wants to meet. Shall I tell her we're willing?"

"Absolutely," Bister said. She took off her work gloves. "But give me half an hour to get cleaned up. I smell like a dead animal."

"I'll tell her an hour," Jamila said. "How about the Hangar? We've eaten there before. It's close and not expensive, and with the crowd breaking their fast after the second sunset it will be busy enough that nobody will pay any attention to us."

"Works for me," Bister said.

In truth, it didn't take them nearly an hour to get there. Bister had changed into a white sleeveless shirt and a pair of clean brown cargo pants. Her hair was still dripping, but it would dry out fast enough in the heat. The Hangar was just that—a massive hangar that had been converted into a restaurant, with open steel struts and an enormous amount of noise. As they were led to a table for three, Bister noted that it was filling up quickly. Either it was a popular time of day to eat, or the holiday had already begun. She said as much to Jamila as they were seated at an industrial-looking surface with built-in screens to order from.

Jamila sat down on one of the not-so-comfortable metal seats. "This place gets a lot of offworlders. I mean, this isn't Menaechmi." She gestured around at the décor and clientele. "So I doubt the holiday has much to do with it."

Bister scrolled through the menu with one finger. "What is the holiday anyway?"

Jamila cocked her head. "I suppose you would be interested in it, given *Sounding Dark* and everything. Personally I don't go in for these old rites, but I suppose they're interesting. The story is that every year the Golden Lady takes a beautiful young man as her consort. That's why you see these pots of grass as decoration everywhere right now, even here. He grows like grain, and then when the year comes to an end he dies. I mean, nobody actually dies. It's grass." She shook her head. "And then there's the whole bull thing. He dies but his soul goes into a bull, and then the bull is killed and he's reborn from the blood to marry the Golden Lady again. So you go round another year." Jamila punched in her order with one finger.

Bister felt a chill that had nothing to do with her drying hair. "Yes," she said. "I'm interested in these old rites." It was as though someone were poking her very gently, saying *Pay attention.* Bister was all ears. "So who conducts these rituals?" she asked casually.

"Beira's where the largest temple of the Golden Lady is. We mostly worship the Lord of the Dance in the south where I'm from, in Ashkela. But here there's a temple and priests and all the rest." Jamila looked up from the menu. "It's part of the trappings of power. The Husband of the Golden Lady has a lot of clout."

"And dies every year?"

"Not literally. It's all symbolic now. He's supposed to give his life as the sacrifice. But it's about politics today. The Guardian of Beira is the current Husband. That's how he got to be Guardian. They had to vote him Guardian after he stole the rite."

"Stole the rite?" Bister frowned.

"Yeah, the word is that he slipped the previous Husband a mickey so he couldn't complete the rite, and there he stood, willing and ready." Jamila looked amused rather than scandalized, which Bister felt also said something about Menaechmi.

There was a low rumble, a different sound from the usual of a large ship landing, and Bister looked up. There was a sudden patter on the metal roof of the Hangar. "Rain," Bister said. Through the wide glass windows that looked across the tarmac, she saw the flicker of lightning in the lowering clouds.

"It often rains at twilight," Jamila said. "That's why this area is arable. The storms come off the sea daily and drop their load when they begin to rise at the mountains. This side of the mountains is very fertile. The back side isn't. It's interior desert and nobody lives there. Well, nobody but the Merrow and they hate everybody."

"Ah," Bister said. She was distracted by the group at the table behind Jamila, who seemed to be having a problem with their menus. Every screen on the table and the call light were all strobing fitfully. There were four of them, two young men and two young women, wearing the light brown shipsuits of the Morriganian Fleet, well-cut pants tucked into low boots. One of the women, red-haired and intense, was leaning close to a dark-skinned boy who seemed upset, whispering something forcefully to him.

"I can't help it," he said, his voice low but enough to carry to Bister. "There's too much ambient. This is a crazy storm."

The dark-haired woman at the table had the seven-pointed star of tactical ranks on her collar and leaned in from the other side. "Lock it down! Boral, get a grip on it."

"I'm trying," the boy said. He alone of the four of them wore no insignia. And that was interesting in itself, wasn't it? Four young people in junior officers' uniforms, and one of them with no rank or specialization insignia.

Bister nudged Jamila's hand. "Take a look at them." The rain was drumming on the roof, and a blast of thunder was louder than the conversation in the crowded restaurant. The lights around the table flickered but nowhere else.

Jamila twisted around in her chair. "Morriganian Fleet? What are they doing here?"

"Morrigan and Menaechmi are friendly, remember?" Bister said. "It must be a small ship. We'd see a ship of the line if there were one here." The lights flickered again, the other table's screens freezing. A moment later came the thunder. The boy's hands were pressed to the table, his eyes closed. For a second Bister thought she saw a curl of lavender along his finger, bright and then suppressed. "He's an electromancer," Bister whispered.

Jamila's eyebrows rose. "They don't let electromancers off

Morrigan."

"They let them off to kick the Calpurnians in the balls," Bister said. "And Perisad said he'd heard the new Warlady had a completely different attitude about electromancers. That she had even raised them to rank. I've never seen one, but…" Bister shrugged. "…doesn't that look like it?"

The boy had his hands flat on the table, taking deep breaths with his eyes closed. The screens had stopped flickering madly and were resetting. The lights were steady. "Maybe," Jamila said.

"The storm must screw him up. That's what he meant about the ambient," Bister said. "There's too much charge in the air."

Jamila looked at her. "How do you know such stuff?"

Bister shrugged. "I keep my ears open." Truthfully, she didn't know. It was just there in her mind. Maybe she'd put it together, or maybe one of the previous avatars of the Lady of the Void had known what an electromancer looked like. It was hard to sort out sometimes. Bister found it easier just to take it as it came.

There was a sizzle and a pop, wiring beneath the next table shorting out, and the fourth Morriganian scooted his metal chair back, cursing as sparks jumped. "I'm sorry!" the boy said too loudly. "I can't stop!"

Electricity in a metal room with metal furniture. Bister got up, crossing quickly to behind him. "Hey," she said quietly. "Still now." She put her hands on his shoulders, like a mother with a fractious child, but what she saw was starry space, the sleeping quiet between pools of light, where even the flow of electrons was slow and stately like long rollers far out to sea. "Still," she said. Void and quiet and healing dark, peace for those who felt the flow, calm and gentle. His shoulders trembled under her hands, and then he was still. The wild energy tamped down. "Calm," Bister said. Cool, quiet dark, like falling asleep in a mother's arms. "There."

The boy looked up at her, a sheen of sweat on his face, but no longer shaking with electricity. "Who are you?"

"Somebody who knows what you are," Bister said quietly. There was someone, someone she had been, someone part of her had been, who had known electromancers. Best to just let it flow through her and not ask too many questions. The red-haired girl's eyes were wide. All of them were just kids, Bister thought. Probably none of them were much more than twenty.

"Yes, but who are you?" he asked. "And nobody knows. We haven't been allowed off Morrigan in…"

"Boral!" the dark-haired woman interrupted. "Cut it!"

"My name is Bister," she said. "I'm Tainted. From Inanna. I'm working freight." All those things were true. Her eyes met his, and she wondered what he saw. "And you are?"

"Boral Hailu-Savarin," he said. "Of the scoutship *Spider*." The name of the ship could hardly be a secret.

"Is this your first visit to Menaechmi?" she asked.

He nodded. "I've never been off Morrigan before."

"Then you should be aware of the weather patterns." Bister glanced back at Jamila. "My Menaechman friend tells me that there are often thunderstorms at the beginning of twilight. I usually have to keep track of it on my handheld when I'm here—I can't remember when the suns rise and set, and the weather can change very quickly here. I expect that will be useful to you." She let go of his shoulders, stepping back.

"Thank you," he said. He had a calculating look, as though he were trying to figure something out.

Bister looked up to see Caralys making her way among the tables, her jade silk apparently untouched by the rain. Her complicated skirts flowed in spikes from hip length to mid-calf, her neckline plunging narrowly to the waistband, provocative but actually showing little. She raised a jeweled hand in greeting when she saw Bister. "If you'll excuse me," Bister said to Boral. "My party is here. I hope you enjoy your leave on Menaechmi." She turned away, aware of the furious whispers behind her as she stepped around the chairs to greet Caralys with a half-bow she'd borrowed straight from Griff. "It's a pleasure to see you again so soon, Gaura."

Caralys looked amused. "And you, Bister," she said. "You do xalepia well for an offworlder."

"Xalepia?"

"Hard woman? Perhaps that is the best translation." She let Bister hold out a chair for her and sat down gracefully, the meshes on her hands attached to jade rings now.

"And you are?" Bister asked.

"I am all hapalia," Caralys said. "Soft woman, sweet and fragile."

"I doubt that," Bister said, regaining her seat. "There is stone beneath sea."

Caralys smiled with what might be genuine delight. "Perhaps."

Jamila gave Bister a look. "Are you seriously flirting with a gaura from a great House? What about Griffin?"

"We understand one another," Bister said. Besides, it was a game. It wasn't going to go anywhere. Behind Caralys she could see the Morriganian kids talking furiously and at last getting their meals delivered. She thought Boral would be all right. He'd just been startled by weather and any bad accident had been averted.

"Unfortunately, I am here on business rather than pleasure," Caralys said. Her face went still as a mask. "I have a principal who has a problem."

"We're listening," Jamila said.

"There is a Calpurnian warship in orbit," Caralys said.

Bister nodded. "We saw it when we came in, along with other shipping. I take it that it's not a welcome guest?"

"You could say that," Caralys replied. "It has seized a Menaechman merchant inbound from Lono, including its passengers. One of whom is my principal's son. The boy is twelve."

"A shakedown," Bister said. That sounded about right. "So the

Calpurnians want a ransom?"

"A ransom my principal is unable to pay. When the Calpurnians do not receive what they want...." She let her voice trail off.

"They'll kill the boy." Bister pursed her lips.

"Or torment him in hopes of extracting the ransom." Her beautiful face was calm, but her voice shook just a little. The child was not merely an employer's son.

"Your own son?" Bister guessed quietly.

"No." Her eyes dropped. "But I know him well." Her expression said what her words did not: *and love him as a son.*

Bister leaned back in her metal chair, a mistake as it scraped loudly on the floor. "Well, let's order some drinks and talk particulars."

Jamila seemed skeptical but pulled up the menu. "Beautiful Poison again and some shared delicacies?"

"Allow me," Caralys said. "It's my party." She ran her hand over the credit scanner and it beeped, apparently reading a code on her ring. She then proceeded to select several items. Jamila's brows rose when she saw the scan go through, but she said nothing.

Bister waited until she finished. "So what did your principal tell the Calpurnians?"

"He told them that he would come up with the currency, of course," Caralys said. "But it would take some time."

"He stalled."

"In essence." Caralys shrugged. "The Calpurnians are Cassian and Junia, the assassins who killed Altissimus Iulus. Iulus returned from the disastrous campaign against Morrigan and was killed by his peers, if you've heard. I presume from the fact they only have one ship and are desperate for currency that they have fled some of the other contenders in what is best described as a fluid political situation. But that is nothing to us. What matters to me is that the boy be retrieved without harm."

Bister wondered if the political situation were indeed nothing to her. She doubted it. But that was how the game was played. You didn't get to the high stakes table until you'd won at the others. "And what kind of concessions are we discussing if we were able to deliver the boy safely?"

"My principal's goodwill."

Bister leaned forward as the drinks arrived, pretty ruby colored tubes with fizzing bubbles in them. "Forgive me, but since I don't even know who your principal is, that's not enough."

"Would you prefer a dizzying amount of currency, or the same in goods for Inanna? Perhaps twelve class-five batteries, industrial refrigeration, water treatment and sanitation systems? And whatever parts and installables are necessary for fitting to your sites?" Caralys asked.

"Useful," Bister said, nodding. She took a sip of her drink, fruity but not too sweet, a sharp red fruit rather than a cloying one. "What are these called?"

"Bull's Blood," Caralys said. "They're traditional for the holiday."

"That's quite a proposal," Jamila observed.

"My principal is very attached to his son." Caralys smiled charmingly. "Would Inanna find those things helpful? Or would you prefer raw currency to split?"

Cutting-edge material was certainly hard to get. Bister had spent six years bringing in that many batteries, not to mention the rest of it. Twelve class-fives would let four more settlements fully power a year-round shelter. Even half of that, given that they took half in currency for Jamila, would be a huge leap forward. "I think we can work that out," Bister said. "The operative question is how to get aboard the Calpurnian ship and how to get off with the child. Jamila, I know you've gotten onto Calpurnia before…"

"That's an entirely different matter," Jamila said. She would have said more, but the attendant arrived with their food at that moment, putting down three small triangular plates, one in front of each of them, and then a tiered server in the center of the table, each tier filled with bite-sized portions arranged prettily.

There were slices of candied oranges and spheres of white cheese wrapped in fragrant leaves, but there were also tiny pastries Bister didn't recognize. "What are these?" Bister asked as Jamila transferred a few pieces to her plate.

"You are very curious!" Caralys pointed to each with a gold-tipped finger. "These are crustacean confit and new cheese. These folded ones are a minced paste of olives and fermented fish." She pointed to the top tier. "And these are sweet rather than savory—lemon and honey."

"Perhaps I should try them all," Bister said. She smiled at Caralys over the pastries. "I do like to try everything."

Jamila snorted. Bister wondered what was bothering her. She seemed to have chilled on this deal more than could be accounted for by Bister flirting with the client. It had never bothered Jamila before who did what with whom if it didn't affect her bottom line.

"Then I insist you try the crustacean," Caralys said. "It practically melts in the mouth."

Bister took a bite of it. It was indeed as good as she said. "Delicious," she said. As soon as her mouth was clear again, she took a sip of her drink. "There might be some reason we could come up with to dock with the warship in orbit. Surely they want to resupply or something?"

"I'm not sure that's a good idea," Jamila said. She didn't look up from her drink.

"They've got to resupply," Bister said. "At least it's likely they'll want to take extra water and oxygen aboard so they can flush their systems. If they're running from the other factions, they would want to supply when they have the chance."

"I don't think we can do that," Jamila said. She looked up, glancing around to where the Morriganian kids were now finishing their dinner and arguing about where they were going next. "Did you know the Morriganian Fleet was here?"

Caralys lifted her chin. "No. And I would have if it were more than a small ship."

"Would you?" Jamila asked.

"Would you expect me not to?" Caralys asked.

"I've never asked which House," Jamila said.

"Does it matter?"

Bister felt there was something going on that she didn't get. "Excuse me? Is there a problem?"

"So the Morriganians have nothing to do with the Calpurnian warship?" Jamila asked. She ignored Bister.

"Not as far as I know," Caralys said. She took a bite of one of the lemon and honey delicacies. "Beira has no antagonism with Morrigan. They are welcome to visit if they choose."

"Beira, not Menaechmi," Jamila said.

"Each city may of course choose its trading partners for itself." Caralys smiled and lifted her drink.

"Of course." Jamila shook her head. "And your House?"

"Simply wants the return of its citizens," she replied smoothly.

Bister put her drink down. "Which is where we come in. So let's work through this."

"I think not." Jamila pushed her chair back. "Gaura, I'm pleased we've been able to do business in the past, but this arrangement is beyond me. I cannot undertake this commission for you. It surpasses my humble capabilities."

Caralys's back was very straight. "I'm sorry to hear that," she said. "I had hoped we could come to an arrangement."

"We may be able to," Bister said. "Jamila…."

Jamila met her eyes. "I'm out, Bister. You want to stay in, you can, but this is too rich for my blood." She got up. "I appreciate your hospitality, Gaura."

Bister got to her feet too. "What is this about?" She looked between Caralys and Jamila, who turned and walked away between tables. "I don't know what her problem is," Bister said. "Truly, Gaura. I have no idea. This sounds like a challenging job, but not impossible. I just don't...."

"You should go after your friend," Caralys said. "Should you decide that you are still interested in the job, I would welcome your contact. Only..." she hesitated, "...soon. We may not have much time."

"I understand," Bister said. "And I am interested. But if I'm going to stay on Menaechmi, I need to get my things before Jamila raises ship."

"May I see your handheld?" Caralys said. "I'll transfer my private contact."

"Of course." Bister held it out and Caralys touched her ring to it, the screen lighting briefly. "If you'll excuse me."

"Naturally."

Bister hurried out of the Hangar. She caught Jamila at the starport service gate. "Jamila! Wait!"

Jamila turned around. "So you decided it was a bad deal too?"

"No," Bister said. "I don't even know what the deal is. We didn't let her finish." She followed Jamila through the gate and onto the tarmac. The rain had stopped and the pavement was slick with puddles.

"I heard everything I needed to."

"What is going on?" Bister demanded. "You've been doing jobs for her before. Why the sudden panic?"

"Because now I know who her principal is," Jamila said grimly. She stopped. "Bister, when she ran her ring over the menu screen it came up unlimited debit on House Melian! That means her principal is the Guardian, Helios Melian!" Bister must have looked uncomprehending because she went on. "The Husband of the Golden Lady. The sneakiest old bastard on the planet! He's tied all the Cities of the Coast up in his intrigues for twenty years and then cheated his way into being Husband. If he's gotten into it with a Calpurnian faction or—Lady help us—the Morriganians, this is the kind of thing that gets people killed. And by people I mean ordinary people, expendable ones!"

Bister thought fast. "So the problem is that he's the person who actually has the power to do what I want him to? Which is get Menaechmi to repudiate the Isolation? That's what I need."

"You have no idea what you're talking about," Jamila said. "Standing between House Melian and a Calpurnian faction is like…" She gestured around the tarmac. "…it's like sitting between two warships and both of them firing at the same time. They may not care if they blow you up or not, but chances are they're going to. I am not getting into any kind of deal that depends on that Merrow dealing straight. He's never made an honest deal in his life."

"Merrow? What?" Bister felt like she was rapidly losing the sense of this conversation. "Is this something about rivalry between the different Cities of the Coast? I know you're from Ashkela."

Jamila shook her head. "I am not working for Helios Melian. And I am not mixing it up with a Calpurnian warship." She took a deep breath. "Bister, I was there when you started one war. I'm not doing it again. I'm raising ship as soon as I can load cargo. You can come with us, or you can stay, no hard feelings. But I'm out of this deal."

"That's fair," Bister said. She kicked at a puddle at her feet. Jamila was clearly scared. And yet rescuing the son of the person who could get her what she wanted made sense. That was how the Lady of the Void worked, at least: she'd give Bister an opportunity if she could, but it was up to Bister to turn it into gold. How long would she have to wait for another opportunity like this? If the Guardian was the one who could effectively destroy the treaty, it would be foolish to throw away the chance to get him in her debt. Bister took a deep breath. "I think I'm going to stay and hear more about this deal."

"Suit yourself," Jamila said. She actually looked worried about Bister. "Be careful. You're used to dealing with the Council on Eresh who are all basically decent people. You have no idea what kind of scorpion's nest you're getting into."

"I'll be careful," Bister promised; and then because Jamila was truly a friend, "You be careful too. You probably know best, but you know I'm stupid."

At that Jamila smiled. "I do," she said, but it was without heat.

"I'll get my stuff and move it to a locker in the port so I don't have to worry about it later," Bister replied. "Would you mind taking some messages back to Eresh for me? I'll write them out now."

"Absolutely," Jamila said.

"And I'll see you on Eresh, my friend."

"I hope so," Jamila said darkly.

Chapter Three

"Assistant, where is the Guardian?" Caralys asked as she stepped into the lift.

Their voice was smooth. "The Guardian has retired."

"Thank you." Caralys addressed the lift. "Eleven." In a moment the door opened into a tiny foyer, one window looking toward the mountain, with no ornament except a chair and a table in front of the window containing a planter of rather wilted-looking grass. She supposed it was time for it to die. There was a single door. She waved her ring to unlock it, and then went down a hall painted rich indigo. To one side the sounds of flowing water and laughter emerged, but she hurried past. The door at the far end opened for her touch as well.

The study was directly beneath the salia, the same bank of windows facing the sea, now overcast with clouds. The walls were sea green, completely fitted with cabinetry painted the same color. A few shelves displayed particular treasures. The cabinet doors that covered the secure business screen and interlink were closed; their cameras would show nothing but the inside of a door. A plush interlocking couch filled most of the room, laden high with pillows and throws in all the colors of the sea. On a day without lowering clouds, it was a beautiful, light-filled room. In Full Night, with stars and sea, it was simply spectacular.

One wall held a huge aquarium, a purple octopus curling out

of its ruby coral to greet her. "Good twilight, Keef," Caralys said, trailing her hand along the glass in greeting as it flowed toward her. "I know you've been fed, so don't tell me otherwise." The octopus matched her hand on the glass plaintively. "I know you're full. Don't give me that sad look." Caralys smiled, spreading her fingers against the tentacles. Then she turned and went through the door at the back of the room into a small alcove with three doors, its deep indigo walls and dim lighting like stepping into night, into the core of the house. She knocked softly on the door directly across. "It's Cara."

The door slid open. The room was tiny, the midnight-sky colored paneling making it look like the inside of a box. There were no lights except for a dim hanging lamp, a bulb within blue glass chased with gold. There was barely room to walk around a bed entirely covered in black linens. Helios looked up from the pile of pillows, his loose robe open down the front. "I couldn't sleep," he said, laying aside the handheld screen he'd been reading.

"I'm not surprised," Caralys said quietly. She sat down on the side of the bed to unstrap her shoes.

"Worrying about Theo."

"Naturally." She kicked the first one off and twisted to get the second.

"I talked to Cassian again." He sighed. "I invited the Altissimi to the holy festival. Needless to say, both of them declined."

"You didn't think they'd be so stupid." The other shoe hit the floor.

"I hoped they would be, but no, I didn't think so." He sat up behind her, unfastening the strap at the back of her neck, the front of her dress falling open to the waistline, baring her breasts. "And how did your meeting go?"

"Not so well. Though I think Captain Ravit's associate is promising. I'm expecting a ping from her." Caralys made her voice confident. There was no point in worrying him more than necessary, especially with the Killing of the Bull hours away. He was already worried enough. "It's progress."

"You know I have complete confidence in you." He unhooked the closure at her waist, and she stood to step out of the dress. "And you have the authority to make whatever deal you need to. I will be incommunicado." There was that sound in his voice, as though he spoke to someone besides her.

"I know. I'll take care of everything." She turned and slid into bed beside him, naked skin on skin and silk. "Now you should try to sleep, my love. There are very long hours ahead."

He gathered her against him, her face against his shoulder, taking a deep breath. "I know you should go, but will you stay?"

"Of course." She must be familiar, soft. She could handle it all. There was no need to put more on him before the rite. And any other secrets she carried needed to stay unspoken for now.

Already there was sleep in his voice, sensuality soothing. "Buying out your indenture was the best deal I ever made."

Caralys smiled against his shoulder. "I think so too." She placed a kiss on his collarbone, feeling him relax.

"Easier to sleep with you here," Helios said. "Even if very wrong." There was something like satisfaction in his voice.

"Very, very wrong." She kissed his chest again, the hollow at his throat. "Such depravity." He took a deep breath, and then another. She pulled the soft knit alpaca wool blanket up over her bare shoulders, felt him sigh into her. "Sleep." Caralys closed her eyes.

Five years ago he'd just become Guardian, elected on the heels of his new holy role as Husband of the Golden Lady. All Beira was divided on whether this was the worst thing that had ever happened or the best. He'd suborned the rite. He was the Golden Lady's chosen. He was vulgar, dishonest, an upstart. He was magnificent, generous, canny. Certainly he was very rich.

The House that held her indenture hated Helios Melian. Since Caralys hated them, it seemed worthwhile to throw herself at him. Curiosity? Revenge? She wondered what he would do if she asked him to buy out her indenture, five years of a gaura's time at market price. It was a ridiculous thing to do at a party on fifteen minutes' acquaintance. The last thing she expected was that he would do it the next day.

"Consider it a demonstration," he'd said the first time he received her in the salia upstairs, dressed in white and gold like his name.

"Of power?"

He shrugged. At fifty-one he was still a striking man, good bones that did not lose their beauty in his angular face. She had always found hapaloi attractive. "Who but Helios Melian would spend a small fortune buying out a gaura's indenture on a whim?"

She kissed his jeweled hand. "I will endeavor to provide good service." She did not look up at his face, trying to make her voice not sound halting. "I was not happy there."

"So I understood from what you said at the party." He walked over to the windows, looking out to the sea, its surface smooth as glass in the long afternoon. "I think you will not find me difficult to please. Most women do not."

Caralys's eyebrows rose. "I heard that your last wife broke the contract when she caught you in the bath with two hapaliae and a disson."

He made some sound that might have been a cough. "There is that."

She put her head to the side, considering. "Though it seems strange that someone as astute as you are reputed to be was silly enough to conduct such sports where your wife would see, if you thought she'd be jealous. It makes me wonder."

"Does it indeed?" He looked out to sea.

"Why would you be careless?"

At that he did turn, leaning back on the window like a boy. "Lyra and I did not suit. She needed money. I needed a marriage with a House with an old name. I hoped we could find ways to satisfy one another, but…." He spread his hands. "And then opportunities arose. This position I now hold—the Husband of the Golden Lady must not be married to any other. Polygamy has never been legal. If I were to be the Husband, I must be unmarried."

"And it would be better if she divorced you," Caralys said.

"It would be better if she divorced me and congratulated herself on the large settlement reached rather than fighting me tooth and nail through the courts," Helios said. "I gave her an uncontestable reason."

"And your custody of Theo and Mia?" Caralys frowned.

He lifted his chin. "I offered her currency or the children. She preferred the currency. Had she been a better mother, she would have chosen differently."

"Do you always buy everyone you want?" she asked.

"I buy access. Access is for sale. Hearts are not." He left the window, walking past the shrine to the Golden Lady, his gold and white long coat whispering against the carpet.

"My heart is the only thing which is mine," Caralys said.

At that he smiled, quicksilver, like a sunbeam through clouds. "Then guard it closely."

As you do? She wondered but did not ask. *Does anyone know his heart?* And there was the fatal prickle of fascination. *What treasure might be in such a carefully guarded citadel? Or is there in fact nothing there, heartless as some say?*

"I didn't buy your indenture to sex you," he said. "You're lovely, but frankly I can buy a great deal of sex for five years' indenture. I need a gaura." He gestured around the salia. "In the last half-year I've become Husband and Guardian. The amount of business has tripled, and there are a myriad of religious duties as well. Between House Melian, Beira, and the Golden Lady's business, it's overwhelming. Additionally, I have four children in the house. Aurore and Dian are twenty-one and seventeen and their mother lives downstairs, but Theo and Mia are entirely mine. They are seven and three, so you can imagine they need quite a lot of attention. I need a charming hostess, someone to manage my schedule, to make all of these bits work." He waved a hand at the house in general. "To make entertaining go smoothly. To coordinate transportation so I'm not left having to take public transportation to the temple, as happened two days ago when Dian took the last house vehicle out to a party without thinking that I needed it."

Caralys stifled a smile. The idea of the Guardian arriving by public transportation was ludicrous.

"Of course I made a big speech about how I shared the life of the city, but that will not happen again," Helios said. "Once is a stunt. Twice is ridiculous."

"I can easily coordinate the house vehicles," she said, trying not to laugh. "And I am well trained in event planning and management. I can certainly be charming to your guests and provide amenities appropriate to their stations." She kept her voice very professional. "Am I to sex them?"

"No." He stopped his circuit of the couches. "You are to plan entertainment, not be entertainment."

And that was a relief. "I am very capable of planning entertainment suitable to any event."

"I thought you might be." That was another calculation, wasn't it? He knew she had an old name. Of course he had learned that she'd been born to an old House that had so little currency that indenturing her as a gaura had seemed a good bargain. But she would know the worth of antique silks, the number of dancers at a feast that would not be vulgar, the amount of food to serve that was generous but appropriate. She would know when the music should be a single professional atthar player and when recorded music was permissible. In short, she could make his controversial office more acceptable to the old elite. He didn't dare dispense with them entirely.

"I will be certain to provide satisfaction," Caralys said. "You may not have my heart, but you have my sincere gratitude."

"I expect that will do," he said.

And so she dressed to please as Full Night came. Since her previous House had claimed most of her clothing as their property, a petty spite, she didn't have a lot of choices. The coral or the lavender? The coral was more daring, the lavender sweeter. It made her look younger than twenty-five, a fresh-faced girl who had no experience of the world. Caralys held each up to her at the glass in her sleeping closet. He had paid for a hapalia gaura. Sweet and innocent it would be.

As she waited in the study, a little table brought in for their dinner, she turned the lights low to set the mood. The window now showed an expanse of sea, a sky thick with stars. Music, she thought. Something soft and low, tender and simple. Caralys smiled. She was finding the place in her head for this, a scene of seduction, a girl waiting for an older lover with anticipation, eager to taste forbidden fruit. Not shrinking; volatile and innocent, hungry for pleasures denied. She smoothed the modest lines of the lavender gown with its front buttons and wide, soft collar, a daring girl's most cherished gown, chosen for her first rendezvous.

When Helios opened the door he stopped short, taking in everything, including her pose on the end of the couch, hands on her knees, eyes wide. Then he smiled, the door shutting behind him. She saw his posture shift, sliding into an appropriate persona. "What have we here?"

"Something that I hope will please you," Caralys said. She gestured at the exquisite morsels of food on the little table. "I confess I don't know what half of these are."

His smile grew. "Perhaps I should introduce you to these delicacies." He sat down beside her, not quite touching, his tunic rich with embroidery. Of course she knew what everything was; she had ordered it all from the kitchen.

"If you would be so kind," Caralys said breathlessly, as though overcome by his closeness. Truth to tell, the pretense wasn't difficult. It was like taking the measure of a partner in the first moves of a dance.

"Do try this one," he said, offering her a morsel. His eyes didn't leave her as she tasted it.

"Delicious," she said, licking her lip just a little to get the last crumb.

He shook his head, an expression of pure delight on his face. "I should pour the wine, unless of course you don't drink wine."

"I am willing to try," Caralys said, leaning just a little closer so that her leg touched his.

"Oh dear," Helios said. "It seems that the kitchen has only sent one cup. I'm afraid we must share." He poured into a silver two-handled cup and lifted it to her lips. "From my own vineyards. A sweet red, like life itself."

The line had the polish of long use, like the cup. But there were some things polish improved. She sipped, raising her eyes over the rim to look up at him through her lashes. His breath caught.

There was a great deal to be said, Caralys thought, for dancing with someone who knew the dance. And it was a dance, a series of movements to be matched with increasing virtuosity as one learned the skill of one's partner. By the time he carefully undid the top button of her gown and she gasped, the thrill that shot through her was real. Certainly it was real as he kissed his way to her hard nipples, artfully enhanced with a skin blush that tasted like strawberries. Certainly his hunger was real as she straddled him on the couch, his head thrown back against the pillows as she rode him, the lavender gown pooling around them. His eyes were closed, lips parted, lost in pure sensation. She did not expect him to tend to her needs the moment he was done, one hand between her legs as she tried to blink beneath long eyelashes and put his hand where she wanted it, grinding against him until she broke.

Afterwards, she lay close against him on the broad couch, her dress discarded. "You're cold," he said, and reached for a thick throw which he tucked around her. Her head on his shoulder, she could feel his heartbeat under her hand.

You have a rescuing thing, she thought. *You want to be the benevolent seducer, the refuge in a storm. You want to save someone. Who did you fail?*

Helios tightened his arm around her. "How was that, Caralys?"

"Lovely fun," she said. She looked up at him without guile so he would know it was true. She had hoped she would find him a tolerable partner. Instead, the dance was well-matched. And then, because she was honest, "I'm not all ultra-hapalia, you know."

"It would be tiresome if you actually couldn't find your own shoes and were late all the time," he said.

"I'm only charmingly late on purpose," Caralys said.

Helios laughed as she meant him to. Then he smoothed her artfully tumbled curls back from her face, sobering. "Your contract is abominably written. It doesn't give me a clue about what you dislike."

That is because my previous employers couldn't care less, Caralys nearly said, but refrained. "I don't like pain," she said.

"Fair enough." He ducked his face against her curls in a quick kiss. "Neither do I. It's not my taste, either to give or receive."

"Now and then, a little naughtiness," Caralys said teasingly. "But nothing serious."

"A little naughtiness," he said. "Part of the dance."

"Yes." It had to be clear it was play. He wanted to romp, to escape life's cares with sweetness and joy. That was easy enough.

"I intend to spoil you utterly," he said. "And perhaps you won't mind some pampering and security."

That was too close to the bone, so she turned her face against his waxed chest, smooth beneath his open tunic. It would be too easy to grasp what he offered with both hands. "If you like," she said lightly. "But perhaps we should finish dinner now." She lifted her eyes to meet his. "We'll need all our strength for later," she said with breathless innocence.

And now, five years later.... Caralys felt her bracelet ping, an incoming message, and extricated herself from Helios without waking him. Naked, she slipped out into the hallway and closed the door, lifting the bracelet to her lips. "Yes?"

"It's Bister," the woman's voice said. "I'd like to meet. I'm interested in working together."

Caralys turned left to her own sleeping closet and opened the door with her other hand. "I'm very glad to hear that," she said. "Give me a moment and we'll arrange a time and place to meet."

Chapter Four

It was twilight, the Greater Twin giving an odd half-light. Boral stopped on one of the closed-off streets, trying to get his bearings. He knew where he was thanks to the map on his handheld. It's just that he didn't know which way he was facing. The crowd was getting thicker and was getting pushed back to the edges immediately in front of the buildings to make room for the parade. Above, there were balconies and rooftop gardens, all packed with people watching the street below.

Red was looking at the clothing advertised on a blinking life-sized screen on the front of a closed shop. "Wow, some of this is expensive!"

"I think those are high-end," Kindy said, scrutinizing an apricot chiffon dress worn on the screen by a dark-haired woman who seemed to be dodging a mysterious man through an exotic market.

"Is that an advertisement or an entertainment?" Paloma asked. "Looks like an adventure to me."

"No, I think it's an ad," Red said. "For the dress?"

"For the guys chasing her?" Kindy said. "Rent-a-mugger?"

'They might do that here," Paloma said.

Now the crowd was getting pushed back as the front of the parade came closer. Some of them raised their arms and started to wail. Boral squished back against Red. A procession came around the corner, or at least it might have been supposed to be a procession. There were no ordered ranks, no identifiable groups. It was just a huge mob of people dressed in white carrying pots of wilted grass. They were weeping, covering their heads with white veils, lamenting. Their voices made a strange harmony, a harmony of grief that cut right through him, wailing as though in deepest mourning. Well, at least Boral assumed that's what people did. He'd never heard anyone scream like that except his mother.

She had been ill since before he could remember. Master Castal-Edo was very gentle with her, and on good days she'd been able to spend some time with Boral as long as another adult was in the room, but she hadn't really been able to raise him. Master Castal-Edo said that terrible things had happened to her a long time ago and that Boral should just be kind. He had been, but as he'd gotten older, she'd gotten scared of him.

The mourners were passing just in front of them now, their eerie wails echoing down Boral's spine like they were weeping for the world. A woman with tears running down her face lifted her head to the sky, makeup making rivulets like scars down her cheeks.

Sometimes she didn't recognize him. Once she screamed like this when he came in the room, huddling in a corner behind the couch, whimpering in terror while he said, "It's me, it's Boral!" over and over and over until Master Castal-Edo came in.

"Eulalia, it's Jauffre," he said, kneeling down beside her without touching her. "If I'm here, you know it's not then." She stopped screaming and Arlaine helped her back to her room. Master Castal-Edo looked tired, or maybe it was something else in the set of his mouth, the lines around his eyes. "Don't worry, Boral," he said. "It's not your fault. Your mother loves you. She can't help it."

Boral nodded and put his face against his teacher's shoulder. He was nearly as tall then. Now he was taller. "There, Boral," Master Castal-Edo said, and put his arms around him while Boral cried.

Boral let out a sob. Nobody noticed in the crowd. The mourners were clutching the pots against them like dead babies. They were screaming like they were in pain. What would it feel like to do that? To just let go and weep and weep? To just scream until the rain came down?

There was a break in the crowd, an organized group coming up behind the mourners, thirty or so city guards with white uniforms and energy pikes in their hands. Boral could feel the current if he tried, though they carried them at port arms, honor guard for the man who walked in the middle. He was older than Master Castal-Edo, dark hair loose and wavy to his shoulders, white streaks at his temples, with an angular face and an unornamented white robe of silk so fine that you could see the shape of his body through it. He held no sprouted grass. His hands were open in blessing.

People threw flowers, yellow and white buds crushed beneath the boots of the guard. Someone lobbed a pot. It shattered on the pavement in front of his feet, clods of dirt and rude pottery scattering, dirt staining his hem. He didn't flinch. "A good death!" people shouted. "Die well!" "Good death!" "Take our sorrow!" "Good death!"

Boral looked at Red. She was crying, grabbing his arm. "Are they going to kill him?"

"I don't know," Boral said. He wanted to cry himself. *He cried that day on his teacher's shoulder, sobbing like a child for everything that must be wrong, for everything that broke his mother into little pieces, for everything that could never be. "You are my father," he whispered.*

Master Castal-Edo didn't let go. "I'm sorry, Boral. I am not your progenitor."

"I know. But you're my father."

"Good death!" "Die well!" They were shouting. They were wailing. A torn yellow blossom bounced off the man's shoulder. He just kept walking, though his eyes turned to the thrower. Dark. Deep. As though he carried the world. His eyes met Boral's for a second. *A sorrow. A secret. A dark place in a corner of the tower where*

Boral hid when his mother screamed. Master Castal-Edo's hand on his shoulder.

Boral let out a sob. Red clutched his arm. "I don't want him to die."

"Good death!" The guards were bringing up the rear. Another group of people came behind, more pots of wilting grass, more veils and screams. Kindy let out a low moan. Boral looked at him. Paloma was standing against the storefront, tears running down her face. Everyone was crying. The whole crowd was crying. The back of the procession passed. Paloma took a deep breath.

"I never…" Red began.

"I've got to get back to the ship," Paloma said.

"Yeah," Kindy said. "The ship."

Boral swallowed. So intense, like it had run through him like current, like a not-quite overload. "You do that," he said. "I think I want to follow the procession."

"Me too," Red said. She was still holding his arm, but it was a good kind of holding his arm.

"I want to see the next part," Boral said. It was like overload. It hurt but it didn't damage. Something like that.

"Suit yourself," Kindy said. He looked shaken. "I'm going to make sure Paloma gets back to the ship without a problem."

"We'll be fine," Red said.

They joined the crowd of people following the back of the procession. It was making its way between buildings toward the plazas along the sea. From ahead they could still hear people screaming "Good death!"

This was really intense. Boral took a deep breath. "Some kind of empathy," he said. Could Dreamers do that? He'd never heard of it. On Morrigan, Dreamers were able to manipulate virtual worlds, but not actual, real people face to face in a city street. Or was this some other gift, something they didn't have on Morrigan? Did different worlds have different gifts? On Morrigan they bred for Dreamers and electromancers and everyone knew that they were supposed to be unique to Morrigan. Was there something else here instead? And what about the Dreamer at the Hangar? Dreamers weren't supposed to be working cargo on Menaechmi.

The crowds along the street got thicker as they got closer to the plazas along the sea. Most people seemed to be following the procession, while others clustered around screens. Ahead was an impressive temple, a huge landing between two sets of stairs that led up to it. The higher stairs were filled with worthies in elaborate clothes. Probably there was some rhyme and reason to it, Boral thought, looking over the heads of shorter people in front of him—like the colors of different Colleges at home were instantly distinguishable to him—but he had no idea what the details meant here. The landing broke the lower stairs into two banks which went down on either side of an alcove whose ceiling was a gilded grid held up by three big marble pillars, white and gleaming, the carvings on them chased in gold.

Another procession came from the temple, a group of mostly women in elaborate white and gold. Some of them were leading a big—well, he supposed it was a bull. Boral had never seen a bull except in books. It was certainly bigger than a cow, and it definitely had male parts.

"Wow, that thing is big," Red said. He hoped she meant the whole bull.

As they reached the plaza in front of the temple, the mourners divided; the honor guard and the man in white passed through them and mounted the steps. Boral and Red were shuffled into the crowd, trying not to accidentally push anyone.

There were huge screens mounted so that people in the back could see. Boral glanced up at them. A woman was making a speech. She was forty or so, with elaborately dressed blond hair and a dress roped with pearls. She had a wreath of gold flowers on her hair, so real looking that they seemed like actual flowers plunged into molten gold. Boral couldn't get a word of what she was saying. He just caught the tone, a prayer or an invocation.

She walked down one flight of stairs as the man in white walked up. Both of them stopped in front of the alcove. She drew a curved, gilded knife. "Oh no," Boral said. The man stood unflinching as she laid the blade against his throat. She said something. He replied.

"I can't watch," Red said.

"I don't think…" Boral began.

The woman turned and went up one flight of steps. The bull was being led out. He wore a wreath of real flowers on his horns, someone holding a halter on each side. They led him onto the grid. He tossed his head, maybe not liking standing on less than solid ground. The man had stepped into the alcove directly beneath the bull's head.

Red buried her face against Boral's back. "Tell me when it's over."

"Ok," Boral said. He didn't look away.

With one stroke, the woman cut the bull's throat. Blood sprayed her white and gold skirts, ran in rivers down over the man who stood beneath as the bull collapsed on the grate, heart still pumping. So much blood. The man beneath turned his face up, eyes closed. It soaked his hair, ran down his face like tears, plastering his robe to his body like a hard rain. On the screen the camera lingered on a close-up, his upturned face, scarlet-washed.

Boral felt a long shiver pass through him, as though the entire crowd had sighed at the same time. *Bathed in the blood of the bull, born in its death….*

Now the woman was speaking again. She handed the knife to a man who stood beside her. He took it ceremoniously. The man beneath didn't move, just stood with his hands at his side, blood from head to toe.

Red had opened her eyes. Her voice shook. "They killed it."

"You eat meat," Boral said. "I don't think this is worse than killing a cow to eat. I've seen you eat steak."

"This is different."

"More like killing a person." The man was still standing there, droplets falling on his face, dark blood on scarlet. "I suppose originally the man was the sacrifice," he said quietly.

"What?"

"There are patterns to cultures," Boral said. "I'm not good at explaining." He glanced back at the screen. "You kind of have to feel it." And he did feel it. He felt the same relief, the same great exhalation as the rest of the crowd. There were no more tears, just the release that comes from crying yourself out. They'd put it on him, all their grief and fear, and he had washed it away in blood.

On the outskirts of the crowd people were drifting toward the side streets. The rite was over. "Wait!" Boral said. "I know her. Bister." As the crowd thinned, he could see the groups on the lower steps more clearly. There was the woman who had helped him damp down the wild electricity during the thunderstorm at the Hangar. She was wearing the same clothes, even. She was making her way through the crowd toward a woman in green who looked familiar. Maybe she'd been one of the other women at Bister's table?

"What?" Red said.

Boral dropped his voice. "That's the woman who knew what an electromancer was. The one in the restaurant. She must be a Dreamer. We have to find her."

"Why do we need to do that?" Red said.

"Because nobody off Morrigan is supposed to know what an electromancer is. We haven't been allowed to go anywhere except under guard for ages. I'm, like, literally the first assigned to a ship and just able to be crew and leave the system! In the last war, the electromancers weren't allowed to go any further than the Belt," Boral whispered urgently. "And other people don't have Dreamers. I mean, maybe priests or something, but not just working on a ship. I have to talk to her. I have to find out how she knows." He grabbed

Red's hand. "Come on."

They wove their way against the flow of the crowd. The steps were emptying by the time they got through. The man was gone, the bull's body still slowly dripping as several priests gathered around. Red averted her gaze.

"...the question is how to manage once I'm in," Bister was saying quietly. "Everything will be locked. I can't do anything quickly, and if they go to jump..."

"Excuse me," Boral said politely. "Bister?"

She turned, her plain white tank top revealing the accretion disk of a black hole on her upper arm. She looked distracted, interrupted in the middle of something important. And then her face changed. She smiled. "Boral. I'm very glad to see you. In fact, I think you are exactly the person I need to see."

"What?" Boral said. The woman in green looked as confused as he felt.

Bister turned to her. "This is an acquaintance of mine, Boral Hailu-Savarin, of the Morriganian Fleet. And his friend."

Red looked confused. "I'm Lieutenant Tyria Zerega-Vesta, Engineering Specialist. I'm pleased to meet you."

"Bister," she said. "I think we saw one another briefly at The Hangar. And this is my business associate..."

"...Caralys," the woman in green said quickly. "It is a pleasure to meet friends of Bister's."

Bister looked a little smug, like someone who has suddenly had the solution to a difficult problem snap into place. "Boral, why were you looking for me?"

He took a deep breath. "I wanted to know how you knew. You know. What you knew. And why you're working freight if you're a Dreamer. I didn't know the Tainted had Dreamers. And a bunch of other things. And why you're glad to see me."

Her brows knit. "I don't know what a Dreamer is, so I have no idea how to answer that question. As to why I work freight, it's to pay for my passage. As to how I knew what you were," she shrugged, "it was obvious. I could see what was happening with the storm and I knew how to help, so I did."

"You just wander around helping random people?" Red said incredulously.

"Isn't that the job of the stranger in the book?" Bister said with a smile. "A mysterious woman comes into town and calls the young hero to action?"

"Who's the young hero?" Boral asked.

"You are, of course." Bister said. "Both of you. Boral, there is a terrible injustice being done which only you can right. I'm asking for your help."

Boral blinked. "What?"

She dropped her voice. "A child has been kidnapped and is being held by the Calpurnian Navy to blackmail his parents into helping them subdue Menaechmi. My job is to rescue the child. I know you have no love for the Calpurnians. Will you help me?"

"I don't…I mean, I fought against the Calpurnians. And it's wrong to kidnap a kid, which is the kind of thing they'd do," Boral said. "I don't know why you want me."

"Don't you?" Bister asked.

Boral took another deep breath. "Well, yes, I guess I do." After all, where would she find another electromancer? "But I'm not who you need. I'm sure my teacher, Master Castal-Edo, would help and he's much better at all of it than I am. I could get him and I'm sure he'd help."

The woman in green, Caralys, spoke at last. "There is no time. If we don't act quickly, they'll kill Theo. I'm sorry, but there's not time to go to Morrigan and back. If anyone is going to be able to rescue him, it has to be done soon." And of course she must be Theo's mother. She sounded like a mother should, worried and scared and trying not to be.

Bister met his eyes levelly. "You are the only person on this planet with your unique talent. Will you at least hear the plan and then decide?"

Red frowned. "We're supposed to be back at the ship in a few hours."

Boral wet his lips. Master Castal-Edo had always said that sometimes you had to make a choice between doing what you were supposed to and doing what was right. Letting a kid get killed by the Calpurnian Navy was definitely not right. He'd been there, had fought that battle, his first battle that he thought was going to be his last but certainly wasn't. And Master Castal-Edo—father, in his own mind—had talked about how important it was to weaken Calpurnia by loosening their hold on client states, something he'd bet the Warlady agreed with. And no, he wasn't supposed to act without orders, but if they were telling the truth, there wasn't any time to go get orders. It would take several days at least, and in war that's forever. "We should hear the plan," he said. "If I can help, I will." Red looked at him like he was crazy. "We should at least listen, right? We're not promising to do it. I'm just promising to listen."

"We should not talk about this in a public place," Caralys said. "It's too dangerous. Come back to my House with me and hear me out."

"Ok," Boral said. He looked at Red. "Come on, Red. We're going to listen."

"I don't like this," Red said, "but the Captain would kill me if I lost you. So I'll come."

The steps had almost emptied. They were a very visible cluster. "Then let's go," Bister said.

"I have a trundle waiting," Caralys replied. She led them down the marble steps and around the building to a side street. A sleek white vehicle waited, small and unmarked. The rear and front doors both winged upward, a driver looking out. There was a single, smooth white seat in the rear. "Please, take the back, my friends," she said. "I'll ride in front with the driver."

Bister got in quickly, sliding over to sit against the opposite window, and Red followed her, leaving Boral squished against the door as it closed. There was a privacy partition that separated back from front. He supposed Caralys and the driver were on the other side of that black screen. The trundle started slowly, cool air coming on fresh and cold with a scent like lemons.

"I hope we're doing the right thing," Red murmured.

"We're going to her house to hear her out," Boral said. "That's all."

"House Melian," Bister said. "You're thinking of a house like a house on Morrigan, just a place where people live. A House is something different on Menaechmi. It's a place, but it's also a family and an economic unit." She glanced out the window at the buildings they were passing. "All of these belong to Houses. They rent or run businesses on some floors and people live on the others. Being without a House, even the poorest House, is the worst thing that can happen to you."

Boral nodded slowly. "Like being without a College affiliation. Nobody will hire you."

"Everybody has an affiliation," Red said. "Every job has collective association. I mean, you can get kicked out, but you really have to do something awful to get kicked out of the College of Starship Engineers."

"Everybody does except electromancers," Boral said. "I was raised in a tower. We didn't even get an Academy until a few years ago. And we're going to get a College, though it hasn't happened yet."

Bister looked at him curiously. "Why do you say so?"

"The Warlady says so," Boral said. "She promised my father."

"Who is your father?"

"Master Castal-Edo," Boral said. "Her life companion. He stood with her at her Investiture."

"Ah," Bister said. She looked like she was adding something up.

Red frowned out the window. "Why does it look like that?"

Boral looked where she pointed. The trundle was passing through different streets, eight- or nine-story stacks of cubes, each one half as high as a room and perhaps ten feet long, connected by exterior stairs and walks. They faced courtyards full of refuse and tents, full of people cooking on portable burners. Children ran here and there, the youngest naked and all of them barefoot. An old woman gave a dog water from a broken plate. People were lined up by a mechanical pump in the middle of the courtyard, each carrying two identical blue plastic buckets. A boy younger than Boral stood along the edge of the street wearing nothing but red glitter body paint and red boots, raising a hand to the trundle. He had hard eyes and his nipples were painted red. Boral looked away quickly. "What is this?" he said.

"Poverty," Bister said quietly.

"I don't understand."

"Of course you don't," she said. "And I promise you it was worse ten years ago. Now they have buckets and a free pump. To be without water in the heat of Day can be death. Those sleeping cubes are cooled. Houseless people, or people whose Houses are bankrupt, can at least sleep two to a crate in the cool for a little currency."

Red looked baffled. "But why don't they have any currency?"

Boral had read about this. "They're extra people. People nobody needs."

"That's one way of putting it," Bister said. "Though I wouldn't. Everyone is valuable, regardless of their utility to society."

"How do you have extra people?" Red demanded. "On Morrigan everybody who is conceived has a place waiting for them! Is this because of free breeding?"

"In a sense," Bister said. "Most places don't decide that people can only be conceived if they're useful. Most worlds prize the freedom for people to choose their place when they're old enough."

"But if that leads to this?" Red demanded.

"There's always a tug back and forth between freedom and safety," Bister said. "Morrigan is very safe and not so very free. Menaechmi is very free and not so very safe."

"We don't have a high social mobility quotient," Boral said. "At least not today. My father made us read a book about that. About how people can change their function and place in society through ability or luck."

Bister looked surprised. "Yes, that," she said. "Can you change your place on Morrigan?"

"Well, I can't," Boral said. "I'm an electromancer. I'm lucky to be out of the tower. I sure can't go do something else, like be an engineer or a stage designer or something. I was conceived to carry on my mother's gifts." He looked at Red, suddenly aware of the anger creeping into his voice. "I'm with the Fleet because I did well in the battle, and maybe that's more than it has ever been before. Haven't you ever wanted to change your place?"

"No," she said. "I like who I am."

Boral took a deep breath, looking out the window. A glittering sign on the nearest building front advertised escorts by the hour. He could guess what that meant from the people his age standing out front wearing almost nothing.

The trundle turned a corner, rolling past what seemed like restaurants or tea rooms on the first floors. Did they have tea rooms on Menaechmi? They looked something like the tea rooms in Holyrood he'd sampled once, just before *Spider* shipped out. The second floor windows were brightly lit too, some in lurid colors. Were those businesses or apartments? Some had balconies open to the twilight, dangling lights and jungles of potted plants.

The trundle made a sharp left, going down a ramp as a door irised open to let them through. It looked extremely sturdy and probably watertight.

"Where are we going?" Boral asked.

"This is House Melian," Bister said. She looked unalarmed. "Its principal property, I would guess."

The trundle stopped in a well-lit garage, the doors opening upward. "It is the principal property," Caralys said, stepping out of the front. "Forgive me, I could hear the conversation in the passenger compartment."

"Of course," Bister said with a sardonic smile. "I should expect so."

Boral felt like something was going over his head. "What?"

"I hope you will come upstairs so that I may welcome you," Caralys said. "And we may talk further."

"I'm delighted to be your guest, Gaura," Bister said with a half-bow, letting Caralys precede her through the doors from the garage into a plush little foyer. Red looked at Boral with an alarmed expression as the doors of a lift opened.

"It's all positive," Boral said quietly. "We're golden."

"An interesting turn of phrase," Caralys said. "Twelve, please."

The lift started up. It smelled faintly fragrant, like fir trees on Morrigan. The door opened and they stepped out into a lavish lobby, with a view of the city in twilight all the way to the mountains that sculpted the edge of the sky. Caralys spoke to the air, or to a monitoring system they couldn't see. "Assistant, Caralys is here with three guests. We will require a water service in the salia."

"As you request," a voice replied.

"Please come this way," Caralys said. "We can talk privately."

"Wait," Boral said. "Who do you work for?"

"Helios Melian, the Guardian of Beira." Caralys stopped in the hallway, waiting for them to catch up. Her voice was low though there was nobody else in sight. "The Guardian's son has been kidnapped. The Calpurnians want to turn Beira into a client state. They've demanded trained spacers and a hundred unwilling young people as recruits for their Navy as well as currency. They'll hurt Theo if they think it will get his father to bend. I will not allow that to happen."

"Shit," Boral said. It all made sense now. It was all big, much bigger than he'd thought. "Yeah."

Chapter Five

Bister followed Caralys into the salia, trying to look like she was used to this kind of luxury. She knew exactly enough to know how far out of her depth she was. Still, doing xalepia required a kind of swagger. She walked like the hottest thing on this or any other planet, a woman who relished the whip hand. Normally this was a bedroom game with Griff. Here, performance was just another social art. Her natural venue was a starport bar, but it was all the same performance.

The salia was on the other side of the building, its windows showing a majestic vista of sky and sea now bathed in soft twilight. It was impossible to keep track of which sun was where, at least without looking at the chart she'd downloaded, so whether it was dusk or dawn was a mystery to her. The deep blue carpet was a shade darker than the couches, a subtle pattern to it that looked like the sea floor seen through clear water. Caralys walked in like she owned it, turning off the screens on one wall and closing cabinet doors over them. "Please make yourself comfortable," she said.

The Morriganian kids were standing by the door like little birds huddling together. Bister sat down on the nearest couch. "Thank you," she said.

A door burst open at the far end of the room and a girl ran in, tangled dark hair and blue tights. "Cara, somebody said Theo was in trouble! It's not true, is it?"

Caralys knelt down, a feat in her high heels, the girl standing in front of her with a demanding expression on her face that only just covered fearful. "No, Mia. It's not true. Theo's ship is delayed. That's all. He's perfectly fine."

Boral and his friend exchanged looks. The girl put her head to the side, her expression softening. "You promise?"

"I promise, darling," Caralys said. "He's just late."

Mia leaned in, putting her arm around Caralys's neck. "I wish he was here."

"So do I," Caralys said. She dropped her face for a moment against the girl's hair.

"Can I come with you to the last part of the rite?" As quickly as weather, she changed course to a wish. "Please? I'll be very, very, extremely good."

"No, my heart," Caralys said. "Your father said not until you're twelve. Are you twelve yet?" Mia shook her head. "And I do not want to hear how some friend of yours is allowed to attend. When you are twelve. This is your father's rule and I will enforce it."

"But do you agree with it?" Mia asked. Boral made some sort of noise. Bister glanced over at him, but he said nothing.

"Yes, I do," Caralys said. "It is too intense for someone your age. You will stay here with your nurse. I was not allowed to go when I was your age, and the situation was less complex." She stood up. "Now, Mia, I have guests of the House that I must meet with. So you must amuse yourself while I attend to business."

"Yes, Cara." The girl gave her a smile that was all charm and quicksilver beauty. "I'm sorry I disturbed your meeting. I was just worried about Theo." She looked at Bister and the Morriganians. "I'm sorry I interrupted you."

"It's perfectly fine," Bister said.

The girl went back out the way she'd come, the door closing behind her. Boral walked around the couch. He frowned. "It's her brother, isn't it?"

"Yes," Caralys said. "Mia is Theo's little sister."

"And he's twelve?"

"Yes," Caralys said.

"Then we have to rescue him," Boral said simply. "I can't let that little kid's brother be tortured to death by the Calpurnians."

Red looked at him incredulously. "Have you lost your mind?"

"Look," Boral said. "There's right and wrong here. Wrong is a kid tortured to get their dad to do something. Right is rescuing him. It's that simple."

Bister nodded. "It is indeed that simple."

Caralys took a step forward. "Forgive me, Bister, but I don't understand the point of involving two junior officers of the Morriganian Fleet. Unless Morrigan is willing to take on Calpurnia again, what is this about? I am happy to talk with any friends of yours, but I am somewhat at sea as to your purpose."

In other words, Bister thought, she couldn't see what possible use they could be. Time for a demonstration. And time to learn just what Boral could and couldn't do. She glanced at the door they'd come in. "Does that door lock?" she asked Caralys.

"Of course." The other woman looked perplexed.

"Could you lock it, please?" Bister asked.

"Yes." Caralys walked over to the door and entered a code in the pad by the door, waiting until it flashed green.

Boral was smiling. Bister smiled back. "Boral, would you unlock it please? Without damage?"

"Sure." Boral walked over, standing by Caralys in front of the pad. He put his hand on the wall just above it and closed his eyes. There was an audible click as the lock disengaged, the pad flashing yellow. He turned back to Bister. "How did you know I could do that?"

"You're an electromancer," Bister said simply. Truth to tell, it was confusing. Part of her was certain she'd seen someone do that before, but at the same time she knew she never had. Having memories that weren't her own was always a little disorienting. It came with being the avatar of the Lady of the Void, she supposed. They must be the memories of a previous incarnation.

Caralys looked impressed. "You can open any lock?"

"Any one I've ever seen, as long as it's electronic," Boral said. "I can't do purely mechanical locks, but nobody has those unless they plan to hold electromancers."

"And you're an electromancer. I thought…"

"That we weren't allowed off Morrigan? It's just changed. And it's supposed to be a secret."

"And now you're telling everybody!" Red snapped. "Boral, we've got to go back to the ship!"

"If you want to go back to the ship, go," Boral said. "I'm staying. I'm going to help rescue this kid. I'm not the kind of person who just walks away and says it's not his problem."

Red took a deep breath. "Fine."

Bister leaned back against the couch arm. "Can you mess up energy weapons?"

He nodded. "I can overload the battery pack, but I can only do one at a time. And I have to concentrate. I can glitch missile systems too, but only if the missile is close. I can scramble any kind of system that I can touch, even if it's just shorting it out."

"Impressive," Bister said.

"And I've done it in battle with the Calpurnian Navy," he said with quiet pride. "When it really counted."

Caralys looked impressed too, as Bister had hoped she would. "So you're a veteran of the recent war?"

"All five days of it," Boral said. "That's how long it took before they asked for an armistice. We kicked their butts so hard they couldn't find them." He came around and sat on the opposite couch. "So I'm your man."

"That's good to hear," Bister said. "Caralys, you said that the Guardian told Altissimus Cassian that it would take time to meet all the demands, but that he could send the currency that Cassian wanted as soon as it could be converted into datasticks in Calpurnian currency."

Caralys nodded. "Cassian agreed that when the currency was delivered he'd release the rest of the passengers and crew of *Light Dancer* exclusive of Theo, but that he would let a representative of House Melian see Theo and confirm that he's unharmed."

"So how's this for a plan?" Bister said. "Caralys, you agree to go aboard Cassian's ship with the currency and see Theo. You bring me and Boral along. Surely you'd be expected to travel with an entourage. People to handle the cargo? That's us. They have absolutely no reason to look for an electromancer. We're unarmed. Boral and I don't look like anybody special. You ask if Boral and I can stay with Theo and take the passengers and crew of *Light Dancer* back in our shuttle. Then we break Theo out from the inside. Easy with Boral to open locks and mess up systems." She glanced at Boral. "Can you do it?"

"What, open Calpurnian locks and glitch their systems? Sure." He shrugged. "That's baby stuff. I could open a lock when I was twelve."

Bister smiled up at Caralys. "Is that a plan?"

She nodded slowly. "Yes, I believe it is." She paced across the carpeted floor. "If this succeeds, we will be greatly in your debt."

"You know what I need," Bister said. "Recognition for Inanna. For Menaechmi, or at least Beira, to throw out the Isolation."

"Wait, what?" Boral said. "The Just War was nearly two hundred years ago. Why does it matter?"

"It matters very much to us," Bister said quietly. "The poverty you see in the streets of Beira is nothing to that of Inanna. Women die in childbirth there. People die from minor infections that wouldn't trouble you for a day on Morrigan. We freeze and we starve and we spend our lives in backbreaking labor. It doesn't have to be. Opening Inanna for trade is the beginning of changing it."

"If you can rescue Theo, Beira will repudiate the Isolation," Caralys said. "I give my word on behalf of the Guardian."

And how much was that worth, Bister wondered. Surely the

Guardian could simply repudiate an agreement made by a gaura. Jamila had warned her that Helios Melian wouldn't play straight. However, backing away from the deal would give her nothing, not to mention leaving the child in jeopardy. No, it was better to go through with it and then try to hold the Guardian to the deal. "Then we have a bargain," Bister said, standing up and offering her hand.

"Wait," Red said. "Boral, we can't commit Morrigan to this."

"I'm not committing Morrigan. Just myself." Boral drew himself up. "Red, I think you should go back to the ship and tell the Captain what's going on. I'm going to help these people. As soon as I get done, I'll be back."

"I'm happy to put one of House Melian's vehicles at your disposal to take you to the starport," Caralys said.

"Let's talk about this more," Red said to Boral.

He looked at Bister. "I'm in."

Caralys took a deep breath. "Then I hope you will enjoy the hospitality of House Melian while I contact the Altissimus."

Caralys went downstairs to the study rather than to her office. It was much more convenient to the salia, and her office was not only down a floor but on the other side of the building, rather than directly beneath. Also, Helios didn't go into her office. She didn't want to leave a message for him on the House net rather than directly on a local instrument he would use. In the study she could arrange communications with the Altissimus and leave her notes at the same time. Helios would surely open his own screen the moment he got home during Full Night.

The communication with the Altissimus's ship was surprisingly easy. She was informed that it was shipboard night and the Altissimus was unavailable. It was agreeable for Caralys to bring the currency at any time, at which point she would be granted access to Theo Melian. The other passengers and crew of *Light Dancer* would be released to her custody, Theo Melian to be held pending the balance. Caralys signed off and set about writing a confidential summary for Helios.

Stars were appearing over the sea, the Greater Twin setting. Full Night was coming. She paused, looking out the window. The sea was smooth, a few ruffles of waves sweeping in gently, impossibly beautiful. *If this is the last time I see it….* She got up, walking around the room, her hand straying over silk and linen pillows on the elaborate couch, over the bits of coral on a shelf. Keef came to her hand when she reached his tank, and she fed him a little even though it wasn't time. It was absolutely possible the Calpurnians wouldn't keep their bargain, but what choice was there? An electromancer at least gave them a hidden blade. She had no doubt Helios would pull whatever strings he could if this went wrong, but she was acutely aware of how few strings he had to pull in this case. Despite best efforts, his financial influence on Calpurnia was limited, and his ability to rein in Cassian and Junia was essentially none. They would be on their own. She had to admit the prospect frankly terrified her.

Caralys sat back down to continue her notes. He must know everything just in case. There could be no loose ends to surprise him in the deals she'd made. A description of the young Morriganians. She wished Helios's oldest daughter, Aurore, was home now instead of several Days hence. Dian wasn't here either, and she didn't know when she'd be home.

She had only been with House Melian two Days when she'd first met Dian. Dian was supposedly away attending to her education, and she officially lived in her mother's apartment on the fifth floor; so Caralys knew of her but had not seen her. So far everyone had been welcoming, or at least polite. Therefore, when she heard loud splashing and yelling coming from the bathing room in half-twilight, when everyone was usually occupied with work, she opened the door to look in.

There were four or five young people splashing in the big tepid pool—naked of course, and rowdily shouting. Two others stood on the edge. One was a young woman wearing nothing but glitter and body paint. Caralys didn't recognize any of them as House members. "What is going on here?" she asked.

A young man turned. "Come to join the party?"

"You must be the new tart," the glitter woman said. "Come here, sweetheart." She grabbed Caralys's arm.

"I think you've made a mistake," Caralys said.

The woman laughed. "Want to see what a five-year contract looks like?" She yanked the shoulder of Caralys's dress, ripping it to the waistline and exposing her breasts.

Caralys screamed. "Help! Somebody!" The swimmers were getting out of the bath, laughing. She kicked the one who tried to grab her foot.

"Dian!" The shout fell like a thunderclap. "Let go of her immediately!" Helios Melian stood in the doorway, his face dark with rage. "Every one of you bratty little tramps, out of my house this moment! Now!" Caralys stumbled to the edge of the pool, her legs not quite under her. "Out!" Helios yelled. "If I have to remove you, I will have every one of your names."

The swimmers scattered except for the young woman in glitter and paint. "Daddy," she said. "I don't see what the problem is. She's a gaura. She's House Melian's gaura. I just wanted to sample her." Face to face and nose to nose, the resemblance was unmistakable, the same sharp features, the same dark eyes. Dian's hair was lighter. And her expression was petulant rather than furious.

"Caralys is not House Melian's gaura. She is my gaura. Her indenture was paid with my personal funds, not the House's." His voice was sharp but controlled. "She is not here for your entertainment."

"Just yours," Dian said.

"My entertainment is none of your business," Helios snapped. "And if that's your idea of entertainment, it's not welcome here. We do not rough up our guests and we do not rip the clothes off people who happen to walk in."

Caralys picked herself up from the pool edge, breathing hard. She held the top of her dress together. It would have to be sewn. It couldn't be knotted.

"She's just for your cock then."

He took a step forward and she took a step back. "That's enough from you. You may be seventeen years old, but I am your head of House as well as your father. You can clear out of here with your spoiled brat friends. You will not spend Full Day under this roof. Nor at your mother's. Not under House Melian's roof! Your behavior is not remotely acceptable."

"Fine." Dian tossed her head. "I'll go. If you're going to be jealous about your trick...."

Helios raised an eyebrow and she fell silent. Another young woman appeared in the doorway, black pants and black shirt, her dark hair cut just short of her collar. "What is going on here? Dian? I just saw your friends running naked and dripping down the hall."

"And you're about to see her running after them," Helios said. "I'll talk to you at a later time, Dian."

"What did you do?" the other young woman asked.

"Why don't you suck up to Daddy, Aurore?" Dian asked. "That's what you're best at." She turned on her heel and marched out the door with her head high.

Aurore put her hands on her hips. "What is going on here?"

"Dian grabbed Caralys." Helios turned. "Cara, darling, are you all right?"

Caralys took a deep breath. She was the newcomer, her position precarious. "Yes. I was just startled."

Helios glanced at the ripped dress. "You have my apologies."

"You didn't do it," Caralys said. She wasn't shaking. Nothing had gone far.

"I'll buy you ten dresses. Whatever will make it up to you," he said. "Dian was out of line."

"She's always out of line," Aurore said. "I've been telling you. That party crowd she's running with are full of bad news."

"Cara, are you sure you're unhurt? You look shaken," Helios said.

"Just a little," Caralys said. "I'd like to go change now." Having this conversation with her dress in shreds was humiliating.

"Of course." He watched her to the door. "Whatever you wish, Cara."

She stopped outside the door, gathering her dignity to walk to her room. There might be people along the way or not. She could clearly hear the voices in the bath.

"Dian again," Aurore said.

"Yes, well, she's young," Helios said. "It's natural to want to have fun and to be a little wild."

"This is more than having fun. That party crowd is a problem. It's all a big joke to them. They're rich and most of them are older than she is. Dian wants to fit in."

"I'll talk to her," Helios promised. "She'll spend the Full Day at some friend's house telling them how cruel I am and I'll lecture her at twilight. She'll apologize."

"But not stop," Aurore said.

"That's enough," Helios said. "Dian will beg Caralys's pardon."

"You seriously paid five years' indenture?" Aurore asked. "That's a lot of currency, Father."

"It's mine to spend, isn't it?" Helios said without heat.

"Look, I know you've been miserable since Lyra left…."

"I don't know what you're talking about," Helios said. "I'm well free of Lyra. I've been enjoying myself."

"What she said about not wanting Theo and Mia because of the blood taint—"

Helios interrupted her. "There's no need to mention that.

They're too young to understand now, but it will be repeated if it gets in people's minds."

"They'll hear it from someone eventually," Aurore said. "Wouldn't it be better to hear it from us? Father, it's just who we are. We're House Melian. People are going to talk."

"I'll give them plenty of things to talk about besides eighty-year-old rumors," Helios said.

"Like spending a fortune on sex? Or having the worst-behaved little merchant princess in Beira?"

Caralys heard Helios sigh. "I do see that Dian could use some focus."

"And less to drink," Aurore said. "She drinks too much. She binges with these friends of hers and they tear things up."

"Perhaps something more consuming of her attention than her studies. The Defense Force? It's small, but a few months of training might break bad habits."

"That could be." Aurore sounded oddly reluctant. "You know, I'd want to be involved if we could arm our merchanters…."

"We're not arming the merchanters," Helios said. "That's a provocation and you know it." He dropped his voice. "Aurore, you've never seen war. You have no idea the suffering it causes. We fight with words. We fight with currency. We fight with influence. But the moment we start fighting with missiles, some people are going to die and others are going to be maimed for life, spending the rest of their days with brain injuries or missing limbs. We cannot do that lightly. We cannot provoke the Calpurnians into a war we will not win."

"Yes, Father."

"Right now we have our hands full with the problems of Beira. You see the situation in the streets. Every Full Day people die from heat or lack of water. You see the difference even a few buckets can make!"

"In Melian blue," Aurore said. "From someone campaigning to be Guardian."

"A bucket is a bucket to someone who needs it." There was the sound of his step on the pool edge. "Trade, Aurore. Prosperity. A rising tide lifts all boats. You say I spend too much money, but what should I do with it? Sit on credit sticks, or spend money from offworld ventures so that it circulates in our economy?"

"That sounds like a very well-crafted excuse for buying a gaura," Aurore said.

Helios laughed. "Speaking of which, I should check on Caralys and see how she is."

That was enough. Caralys turned and ran swiftly down the hall, through the study and the alcove to her room. He couldn't catch her listening at doors. She barely made it into her sleeping closet before she heard his step. There was a knock on the door. "Caralys? Are you all right?"

She made her voice bright. "Yes! Just changing! I'll be out in a minute." She heard his steps going away and took a deep breath. Changing clothes. Yes. There was no point in thinking about anything but the next move. Caralys chose a simple sheath of blue linen, fine and well-cut but without embellishment. Then she went out into the alcove and across to the study.

He was standing by the window, waiting but trying not to look like he was waiting, an oddly charming gesture. He turned immediately. "Caralys, I want to tell you again how sorry I am."

"You didn't do anything." She joined him at the window. It was early in Full Day, the water white-capped, shining with dazzling flecks of reflection. "Believe me, I got used to far worse in my last House."

Helios frowned. "It was still an intolerable way for you to be treated."

"And you put a stop to it." She sat down on the end of the elaborate couch. Best to confront things directly. "I did not know that you had purchased my indenture personally, rather than for House Melian."

"Well, yes." He sat down an arm's length away. "Very useful for many purposes."

She could not think of a single one. "A very expensive infatuation." Caralys met his eyes. "Like throwing gold in the sea."

He smiled, that narrow smile that was endlessly arousing. "You throw gold in the sea for luck."

An expensive infatuation indeed, and he was, as he said, easy to please. At least for her. She could see the pulse jumping in his throat, eyes on hers, caught in her net. "Are you a lucky man?" she said, leaning in.

"Very lucky." He leaned closer still. His lips parted.

"Maybe some of that luck will rub off on me." Centimeters apart. He smelled like cedar and salt, desire fresh as blood.

"I expect so," he said almost against her lips. They touched, warm and sensual and so very thorough, a kiss to begin and end. *No wonder the Golden Lady loves him*, Caralys thought. *What woman can resist where a goddess falls?*

They were on the sofa, his arm around her and her in his lap when she came up for air. "And when infatuation ends?" she asked. Five years was an impossible time.

"I will make certain you don't regret me."

He was looking at her that way again, and his words made no sense. Why would he care what happened to her after he moved on? "Why?"

Helios's expression said that she'd asked something incomprehensible. "Because I want you to be happy." It caught in her throat. Whatever words she'd planned were lost. He bent his head, looking up at her, that smile again. "Lovers are like flowers, not oysters. I can't just pry your heart open with my oyster knife."

And that was absurd, silly enough that she laughed. "Your oyster knife? That line is probably older than I am!"

He laughed too. "It is. And I'm quite a bit older than you are." Twenty-six years. She had counted, of course. If her initial request that he buy her indenture had been impulse, she had made up for it with research since then. He lifted her hand to his lips. "Are you an ambitious woman, Caralys?"

Being hapalia required that she blink and say no, that she had no desire except to give sweet pleasure. And yet somehow he invited too much truth. "I don't know," Caralys said thoughtfully. "I've had so few choices, I've never considered what I might want if I could have anything."

His brows quirked. "You are very young. Sometimes ambition comes on later in life." He kissed her hand again, lips soft against her fingers. "You might give it some thought. What would you want if you could indeed ask for nearly anything and get it? Who would you want to be if you had opportunities?"

Once again, being hapalia required that she say she wanted nothing but him. And yet. She wanted him and maybe lots of things more, things she didn't even have names for yet. And if she said she wanted him, it was true. "You are fascinatingly complex," she said.

"So I've been told." Helios's smile deepened. "It's one of the nicer things they say about me."

"One of the truer?"

"Many of them are true, including ones you'll like less."

There was no answer to that she could give, so she kissed him and drew him down beside her on the couch to make love in the bright light through the window, sea reflections shifting on the ceiling, as though both of them lay beneath the waves caught in a vast, golden net.

And now, not quite five years later… Caralys sat in the same beautiful room, though the light outside was different. What else to say in the note? Not the thing she held closest. Now was not the time. No, she would end it thus. "We are leaving directly from the Marriage to the starport, so I will not speak with you. May fortune favor you, my love."

Chapter Six

The sun was setting into the sea. A servant had brought refreshments, and then returned with two basic blue jumpsuits, one for Bister and one for Boral. Bister noted the honeybee of House Melian embroidered on the front pockets. "We'll look like anonymous retainers," she said to Boral. He was having a heated conversation with his friend by the window and didn't look up.

Bister paused instead by the statue of the Golden Lady. There was a similar little shrine on the Glitter Rim in Eresh. After all, she was the patron of commerce. Bister had been past it a thousand times, but she didn't think she'd ever made an offering. Her lady was the Lady of the Void. The Golden Lady's worship was unfamiliar to her. Still, there were some things that would be acceptable, and one should always show respect for the gods. Bister bent her head. *Golden Lady,* she thought, *I am not your servant, but I ask your blessing upon those who are, especially on those who now set out to tread my Lady's realm. Please grant your blessings to those who love you, and on me in this temporary service to you.* Bister took a deep breath and opened her eyes.

There was no sense of presence, just the usual calm about a well-used shrine. So be it. That was pretty much what she had expected. Meanwhile, it was time to cut short this argument. "Boral," she said. "You and I should ask if there is a place we can change into these uniforms."

"Boral," his friend said, clearly still trying to talk him out of it.

"I think you should go back to the ship, Red," he said. "Tell the Captain what's happening. But I'm doing this. It's the right thing to do, and I'll be fine." He looked at Bister. "Yeah, we should get changed. I suppose it's all right to leave my uniform here and change back when we get back."

"I think so," Bister said. He seemed to have acquired confidence with the mission. Maybe he just needed to know that what he was doing was right. A good kid, she thought. She'd have been proud if her son had turned out this way. It didn't even hurt to think that, not more than a little. It had been almost sixteen years. "Let's ask the attendant."

The attendant ushered them to cubicles down the hall, and Bister changed quickly. There was no point in taking anything with her, not even her ID. That would betray her if anyone asked for it. If she had none, she'd just say that was House Melian's orders. Boral would be the same. And absolutely nobody would be looking for a Morriganian electromancer.

When she came out of the cubicle, Caralys was coming down the hall. She had changed clothes too. Her gown was the same shade of blue, a transparent overlay over darker panels of the same color which covered breasts and genitals on the diagonal while leaving the rest half-concealed. A half-cloak of the transparent material wrapped around her left arm, her right arm bare and ornamented with golden bracelets. Her hair was pinned up elaborately and bound with a golden snood.

Bister must have looked stunned, because Caralys smiled. "Yes?"

"Just admiring your gown," Bister said.

"The blue is House Melian," she said. "And the formality is that we must attend the last of the rites in the holiday cycle before we head to the starport. If I am absent, Melian's rivals will take due note, and we do not wish to cause alarm. It's best if this can all be handled quietly."

"I agree," Bister said.

"The driver can drop us, take the Lieutenant to the starport, and then return for us." Caralys proceeded down the hall to the salia, Bister trailing behind. She certainly looked like the kind of woman who had a bunch of attendants. There was definitely something alluring about the combination of femininity and power, but then Bister had always liked what the Menaechman called hapalia. Her mirror, she supposed, though her attempted relationships with that particular look had always crashed and burned. To be fair, all her attempted relationships had crashed and burned except Griff. Maybe they just deserved each other.

And now Caralys was saying something and she'd missed the first part. "...if you stay with me entering the seats, there will be standing room behind. Unfortunately, the seats are reserved."

"Of course," Bister said, as Boral and his friend joined them. "And it wouldn't be in character for us to sit with you if we're House retainers." She looked at Red. "Caralys was saying that the driver would drop us and then take you to the starport. I appreciate your patience with all this."

"I'm just worried about Boral," Red said.

"I'll be fine," Boral said with a grin. "Remember, I was born with lightning in my hands."

"Oh, please don't say that out loud!"

"Let's go," Bister said.

Caralys called for the lift. Her fingers in their gold hand meshes tapped impatiently as they descended, though her face beneath the makeup was as impenetrable as a mask. It was a larger trundle this time, blue with House Melian's honeybee on the doors, an official vehicle rather than the private, unmarked one they'd used earlier. It was also exceedingly plush inside with plenty of room for everyone. As Caralys arranged her skirt, Bister wondered if the gold ankle bracelet in the shape of a snake was merely jewelry or concealed some electronics. Or possibly it was symbolic. These were both interesting and important things to know. "So what is this particular rite?" she asked.

Caralys shifted on her seat, her eyelids shining with fine blue sparkles. "This is the last and most important public rite in the worship cycle that began last Full Night, sixty-four hours ago. It's the marriage of the Golden Lady to Her chosen Husband."

"After he was bathed in the blood of the bull and reborn?" Boral asked, and Bister blinked. She hadn't expected him to get that.

Caralys nodded. "Exactly. He took on the sorrows of the city and carried them with him to the grave. Then he is reborn from the blood, as we are all born in blood, and once again becomes Her Husband."

"So he makes vows and things like that?" Boral asked interestedly.

"Yes," Caralys said. "He promises to do Her will temporally as Her priestess does Her will spiritually. And he promises that he will protect Her people with his life if necessary."

Bister nodded. "Of course."

The trundle was making its way through a crowded street now, guards letting it through when they saw the honeybees on the doors. They moved a barrier and let the trundle pull up to the edge of the temple plaza.

Caralys raised her head. "Don't say anything. Just follow me quietly and stand at the back. And don't be disconcerted." The last was addressed to Boral. Bister supposed she looked less easily disconcerted.

The doors opened. Caralys stepped out into the light of five or six handheld recorders, clearly credentialed press allowed inside the barriers. She graced them with a smile as they recorded her from all angles, a woman with teased blond hair talking into her handheld, apparently for live coverage. "And now we have Caralys

Sardai i Melian, Gaura of House Melian, wearing Acritoch by Ermen." Caralys turned and dipped, a sweet smile on her face. The woman went on like Caralys couldn't hear her, or maybe that was just the style. "She's been Gaura to Helios Melian for five years, despite all the juicy rumors about a certain disson architect two years ago! They've prospered. So has she. It makes one wonder, doesn't it?" The woman shoved her handheld at Caralys. "Do you have anything to say, Caralys?"

Caralys blinked, the sparkles on her eyelids catching the light. "I'm just so honored to be here! What more can I say? It's a wonderful night and I hope everyone watching at home celebrates in their own special way!" She gave a naughty and cute wink.

"And what about the rite? Any concerns?" the woman asked, following her along the path toward the temple, Bister and Boral trailing.

Her eyes were wide. "I just hope that all the drapery doesn't catch fire like it did last year!" She giggled. "It's too hot!"

"Yes, that was unfortunate…." the woman continued, galloping after them while Caralys sailed past the guards on the steps. They let Bister and Boral through, but stopped the other woman, who turned back unconcernedly to catch the next person.

It was dark, blessedly dark, for a few paces up the stairs and into the side door of the temple. "What was that?" Boral whispered to Bister. Whether he meant the reporter or Caralys's apparent personality transplant, there was just no explaining. She shrugged.

They followed her through a door held open by a woman in white and red uniform with an energy pike, who apparently knew Caralys on sight, and into a lower corridor of the temple. "Just stay with me," Caralys whispered.

The corridor opened into a crowded gallery full of gorgeously dressed people, and Bister stepped a little closer to Caralys, scanning the near crowd. She knew how a bodyguard should behave. She certainly looked like one.

The walls were dark red, covered in plush material broken by strips of glittering lights from ceiling to floor. A strange sculpture of what might have been leaves as big as people cast in silver stood in a gallery with ramps going up. Caralys exchanged a few words with this person and that, always managing to keep moving. Bister kept scanning the crowd. My, there were some expensive trinkets here! It was a pity that none of them were going to get lost during the evening. And poor Boral didn't seem to know where to look with all the beautiful bodies on display, artfully framed in luxury fabric. He kept running into people because he was looking at his feet.

A long ramp curved upward. Caralys put a graceful hand on the rail as they went up, presumably because her shoes looked nearly impossible to walk in. Four more people greeted her. The gallery above was just as lavish, the walls green marble. It curved to the left, curtained openings on the right.

A beautiful disson in immaculate grey pants and a plum hat with a cockade of feathers embraced her, and Caralys patted them on the back. "I'm surprised to see you here," she said quietly. "I thought you didn't have patience for this kind of thing."

The disson smiled, looking delighted. "I don't, usually. But a friend invited me. How is Helios?"

"You're about to see," Caralys said. "You know. He never changes. Is this a friend or a friend?"

"A friend but hopefully a friend soon, if you know what I mean." They blushed.

"Well, I hope it goes magnificently," Caralys said. Her expression held real affection, and she kissed them lightly on the lips. "Sweets to the sweet."

"Twilight drinks sometime and we'll catch up?"

"Yes, absolutely," Caralys said. "And do take care of yourself, Valeri. Leave me a ping letting me know your schedule."

"I'll do that after Full Night." Valeri blushed again.

Caralys let go, sailing off again along the gallery, Boral and Bister scrambling after. "Your former lover or his?" she asked in a low voice.

Caralys looked amused. "Both."

"If I'd known that was the way it was played, I'd have worn my good boots," Bister drawled. Caralys laughed, as Bister had meant her to. She led them through one of the curtains to the right, down two steps beyond, Boral following behind looking as though his ears were burning.

It was a curtained box in a surprisingly small space, only three across each side and three up and down, with this one in the middle tier, thirty-six boxes in all, around four sides of a dais in the center of the floor. Four golden statues were at each corner of it, the Golden Lady life-sized, a lit firebowl at her feet. The nearest one held a basket of fruit and olive branches, while the next one had waves lapping at her skirts, a golden net spilling fish. All symbols of plenty, Bister thought, aspects of prosperity and wealth. Maybe Inanna needed a bit of the Golden Lady. In the center, framed in transparent golden curtains, was a large square couch piled with gold and white pillows.

There were three plush red chairs in the box. Caralys settled into the one on the right. "Who are the other two chairs for?" Boral asked.

"Not us," Bister said.

"They're for Aurore and Dian Melian," Caralys said. "But Aurore is offworld and Dian never comes to these things." For a moment her voice caught. "Theo would have come with me tonight. He's turned twelve. It was supposed to be his first time."

"He will be here next year," Bister said. She didn't quite put her hand on Caralys's shoulder. That wasn't appropriate for a bodyguard, though leaning in to talk certainly was. "We'll get him back."

"Yes." Caralys's perfect lips set in a determined look. "I have confidence in you. I'm not entirely certain why."

"Perhaps you know a capable person when you see one," Bister replied. That was no more and no less than the truth.

A group of musicians were finishing setting up by the lower bank of boxes, and the first notes inserted themselves into the murmur of conversations. The conversations slowly muted, the music coming up, flutes and stringed instruments Bister didn't recognize, a light, persuasive tune that turned round and round on itself. Three women appeared from one side, the lights overhead dimming so that only the lights on the couch remained, and the flaming firebowls. It was a warm, intimate light, yet bright enough that the women must not be able to clearly see the boxes above in shadow.

The one in the center stepped out to speak. She was in her forties, Bister thought, tall and blond with her hair held up with a pearl-encrusted comb, wearing a thin golden robe that reached the floor.

Boral poked Bister. "Is this going to be a play?" He looked eager. "I've never been to a play."

Bister pulled him to the back of the box where they were hopefully less audible. "In a sense," she said. "It's sacred drama. It's a rite so it's somewhere between a play and a religious experience." She had no idea if that would make any sense to a boy fresh-come from an electromancer's tower.

"I've read a lot of plays," Boral said.

"Not like this one," Bister said. She turned back to the center.

The priestess in gold had finished speaking and the other two were anointing her, oil glistening on her forehead. Her robe opened completely down the middle, and Boral sucked in a breath as they anointed the hollow between her breasts and then her navel. About her, the strangeness grew. Bister smiled. The priestess's posture changed, her face shifting from the lines it usually wore, as though someone else stood inside her. She made no gesture, and yet the air around her crackled with power. Bister could feel it, dangerous and yet tightly held, wild as the sea and yet as generous. Her eyes sought Bister's, though she could not possibly see her with the lights.

The Golden Lady is the child of the Lady of the Void and her lover, the Lord of the Dance, something whispered inside her. *Holla, daughter,* Bister thought, and the part of her that was her and not her laughed at the Tainted expression. The priestess smiled, her chin dipping just a little. The other priestesses bent, parting her robe and anointing her bare mound. Boral made a little noise.

Now a man approached from the other side, the lights gleaming off his dark hair which just brushed the collar of the robe. He wore an identical robe in white, and his eyes were on nothing but the priestess, his step firm and confident, a little smile on his face. The priestesses with the oil turned, coming now to anoint his forehead.

"That's the man with the bull," Boral whispered furiously. "The man who was washed in the blood. And she's the woman who killed it."

"Yes, Boral," Bister replied. She'd missed whatever the priestesses asked him before they anointed him, probably promises to do the Golden Lady's will. Now they were parting his robe, anointing chest and belly and his half-ready phallus. He tilted his head back, the smile pulling a little to one side, as though he slid into something that was pure bliss.

The high priestess spoke. "Return to me," she said simply. With one hand she unfastened the clasp at the throat of her robe, letting it fall to the floor in a susurration of silk. She stood naked in its golden puddle.

"I return," he said, and let his fall as well.

They stepped toward each other, meeting at the edge of the couch in a kiss, his hand caressing her hip, her hand opening on his back. It was utterly beautiful. A collective sigh filled the room. Watching them touch, flesh to flesh, mouth upon mouth hungrily as though they had starved for one another a year, Bister felt every bit of longing. It was like that when she came home. Was that what it looked like when she and Griff lay under the stars? She could almost feel his hands on her hair, on her breasts, as she watched the Husband kiss his way down her neck, as they sunk down together on the couch. Some people, she thought, would have selected a young man and woman, twenty and physically perfect, but this primal energy demanded more. And there was no flaw, not the priestess's stretch marks, not the Husband's love handles. All bodies were perfect, and this was surpassingly beautiful.

Boral was watching with wide eyes. Caralys sat forward in her seat, her lips parted just a little, her eyes never leaving them. Long and slow, to the rhythm of the music, its tempo setting the pace. The lights illuminated. Surely there were cameras, but the sacred couple seemed oblivious to them. He gently drew the comb from her hair, a cascade to her waist, and laid her back on the silks, her eyes closing in bliss as he sought the depths between her legs with his mouth.

"Woah," Boral whispered. Bister was finding him somewhat distracting.

"Have you never seen people make love?" Bister whispered back. On Inanna a boy his age had certainly seen couples around the autumn fires, even if he'd not yet gone into the night himself with some girl or boy.

"Not even in a vid!" Boral said. "We didn't have mature vids in the towers! Master Castal-Edo complained about it all the time!" Bister carefully avoided looking down. Boral was embarrassed enough as it was.

"Then watch and learn," Bister said. Honestly, what did they teach children on Morrigan?

Now priestess and Husband were side by side. She kissed his throat, said something too low for the microphones, something that made him laugh. Lazy, sensual, as though underwater, framed by the golden curtains, firelight flickering on their skin…. The statues of the Golden Lady faced out, promising bounty to those who watched the living personification of Her marriage. Touching, coaxing, her breath coming faster as his hand slid between her legs. He was hard now, not a big man but well-hung, holding back, tightly controlled as any vid star who had to make it through five trial filmings.

Bister took a deep breath to cool off. Her private parts were throbbing against the seam of her pants, and no relief anywhere. She was caught in this net, deliciously, amazingly caught. Could even the Lady of the Void be snared by flesh? *I always am*, something whispered inside her. *That's the story, dear one*. And it was, of course. The Lady drawn to her lover, to warm, life-giving worlds.

The priestess threw her head back, eyes closed, mouth gasping. Not quite. Not quite there. But there was no hurry. He'd give her more. Her body moved against him, his hand between, putting pressure just where she needed it. The audience seemed to hold their breaths with her. Bister put her hand to the doorframe to hold herself up.

There. Her head snapped forward, hips moving wildly, as just at her height he thrust into her. And now it was his eyes that closed, her hands clenching on his buttocks, a steady rhythm, his head down like the bull.

Caralys made some tiny noise, her hands open against her skirts, her eyes never leaving them. Bister resisted the urge to grind against her pants' seam. It would upset Boral no end. No doubt in other boxes people were less restrained.

The music rose. The musicians were working in time to it, or perhaps they followed the music like dancers. The moment was easy to see, a long thrust that didn't stop, her hand opening as though to pull him closer. A collective sigh ran around the room like a mutual orgasm.

There was a moment of pause, and then they tumbled together on the silks. She brushed her hair out of his face and he laughed. Sweat shone on his face. He looked like a runner who had crossed the finish line first, the defending champion winning again. The priestess was smiling, her leg hooked over him, his arms around her.

"Blessed Khreesos," Boral said. He swallowed hard. "They actually…." He waved his hands.

"This is the Sacred Wedding," Caralys said. "What did you expect?" Her face was more or less composed.

"The man—the bull—this." Boral seemed to be having word problems. "Who is he?"

"That is Helios Melian," Caralys said.

CHAPTER SEVEN

The ride to the starport was quiet. It was Full Night. People spilled out of cafés and taverns to tables along the street, celebrating the Marriage with friends and lovers and family. Bright strobing lights in all colors chased one another, promising delight. They reflected off the tinted windows of House Melian's trundle. The public part of the rites was over. Caralys had a shuttle waiting with the currency for the Calpurnians. The trundle would take them to it, then go back to the temple and wait for Helios. It would certainly be several hours before he arrived home and read her notes. She wished she could wait for him, but obviously that was not an option. This had taken long enough as it was. Theo would be frightened.

"Everything all right?" Bister asked.

"Just worrying about Theo," Caralys replied.

She had been five Days at House Melian before she met Theo. She'd not seen Dian again, though no doubt she would. Aurore had been distantly polite, as one is to someone who isn't expected to stay long.

It was Full Day, dropping toward the Greater Twin's setting. They'd gone to sleep on the couch in the study. Sleeping was utterly vulnerable, as private as toileting on most worlds. Small children might be put to bed by an adult, just as little Mia was taken to the bathroom by her nurse. The sick or the very old might sleep in a room with someone to check on them, but for adults to share a sleeping closet was as strange as sharing the bathroom—a very specialized kink indeed. Sex in beds one intended to sleep in was something most people found slightly disgusting. After all, there were plenty of appropriate places for sex.

Sleeping on the couch wasn't quite that bad. After all, it was accidental and nobody needed to know. And yet they slept on the couch comfortably enough amid the pile of sea-colored pillows, a generous white knitted throw drawn up over them, his left shoulder for her pillow, her bare breasts against his side. The setting sun came in through the window, making a warm patch across their feet. Caralys stirred when she heard the side door open.

"Daddy?" a small voice said.

Helios grimaced. He sat up bare-chested, managing to keep the throw around his waist and most of her behind him. "What is it, Theo?"

A boy stood in the doorway, with dark hair and dark eyes in a sweet face. "Will you play Tailors and Towers with me?"

Helios scrubbed his face. "I will, but not right this moment, Theo. And do you remember that you are supposed to knock before you enter a room?"

"It wasn't locked." Theo looked unconcerned. "When will you come play?"

Helios looked at the screen. "In twenty minutes. Give me twenty minutes."

"Is that Caralys?" He craned his neck, curious.

"Yes. Now go on. I will be there in twenty minutes." The door closed and Helios got up. "Shower. Clothes. Tailors and Towers."

"I should not have been sleeping on the couch," Caralys said. She squirmed with embarrassment. For a child to be aware of a co-sleeping kink… "I'm so sorry."

"You are perfect." He bent down and kissed her. "I forgot to lock the door." And with that he was off to the bath.

It was some hours later, in Lesser Twilight, that Theo cornered her in the family dining room. She'd dressed casually—a loose knee length dark blue linen dress and slip-on sandals – perfectly decent for the House. She was eating an orange and an almond cake, drinking coffee thick with cream, watching the financial news stories on the table's screen, when Theo plopped down in the chair across from her. "So you're Caralys," he said, folding his hands in businesslike fashion on the table.

"Yes," she said. She muted the screen. "I am." She steeled herself.

"My father says you're going to stay for five years."

"That's what my contract says, yes." She felt she was on safe ground there.

"If you're not leaving in a Day or two like the rest," Theo said, "am I supposed to call you Mommy?"

Caralys looked around the room, but there was no one to rescue her. "No. You can call me Caralys."

He seemed to consider this. He had exactly his father's eyes, a brown so deep it was nearly black in the right light. "May I have some of your cake?"

"Yes." Caralys pushed the plate toward him. "We can share."

"That's great." He broke a piece off with his fingers. "Five years is a long time," Theo said thoughtfully. "I suppose that's why he didn't put you in a guest closet."

"I'm not in a guest closet?" Her sleeping closet was small but beautifully appointed, presumably next to Helios's own for convenience. He'd told her to buy whatever she wanted, and she'd indulged herself with sleek bamboo sheets and alpaca blankets in purple and gray.

"That was my mother's room." Theo shrugged. "But she left a long time ago when Mia was a baby. Nobody's stayed there since. At least," he said with scrupulous honesty, "that I remember."

Certainly nothing in training had given her any idea how

to have this sort of conversation. They seemed to expect that employers' young children were more or less invisible. In the old Houses that was true. She'd rarely seen her parents, at least when they were sober. "Well, I hope we will be friends."

Theo gestured to the cake. "We already are. You broke bread with me."

"So I did." Caralys smiled. "How old are you, Theo?"

"Seven," he said. "And Mia's three, which is why she's still learning to use the potty. I like that."

"Excuse me?"

"Nurse has to take her to the potty and she takes forever. So I run up and down the hall calling all the lifts. If you run fast you can hit the ones at the far end, then run to this end and call the utility lift. When the ones at the other end open, they stay open long enough for people to get in, so if you run really fast back you can hit the call before they leave and then they'll open again and wait again. And then you run back to this end and do the same with the utility lift. And Nurse yells 'Theo, what are you doing?' and you yell, 'Nothing!' and you can keep it going for a really long time because that's how long it takes Mia to poop." He looked proud. "And you can tie up all the lifts in the House."

Caralys burst out laughing. "And does your father like you to tie up all the lifts in the House?"

He shrugged. "Of course not. But he doesn't know, does he?"

"Not until he's left waiting for one," Caralys observed.

Theo shrugged again. "He won't be very mad. He never is." He took another big chunk of cake. "Caralys, what's a Merrow?"

She took a quick drink of her coffee. "Why do you ask?"

"It's a thing I heard somebody say. I wondered if it was a bad word."

"It's not a bad word, though some people use it like one," Caralys said. "The Merrow are the people who live in the desert. Hundreds and hundreds of years ago they decided to leave the

Cities of the Coast because they believed that the Third Lord wanted them to. They have their own settlements and their own rules, and they don't interact much with us."

"Why not?"

Caralys considered how to best put it. "They think we're decadent and cruel, and their Third Lord says none of the other gods are real. So they went off to live according to their own code. They have the entire center of the continent and we have the shore, as far as the opposite slopes of the mountains."

"But ours is nicer than theirs," Theo observed.

"That is true. But they are the ones who chose to go live in the desert," Caralys said, "hundreds of years ago. Sometimes Merrow decide they don't want to anymore and then they come into the cities. But that doesn't happen as often as it used to."

"Because we hate them," Theo said, stuffing a piece of cake in his mouth.

How to make something so complex simple enough for a child? "We don't want to follow their rules, and they think their rules ought to be followed by everybody. So now when Merrow come to Beira they have to follow our rules if they want to live here, just as we would have to follow their rules if we lived there." She pinched off a piece of the cake too. "In the past there was a lot of violence. But that hasn't happened in a long time."

"So calling somebody a Merrow is a bad thing?"

"Yes," Caralys said. "It's not a nice thing to say, and you shouldn't say it. When people say that, they mean you're an unwashed savage who wants to burn the temples and destroy the way we live, or that your ancestors were fanatics. So you mustn't call anyone that. It hurts people's feelings."

Theo nodded. "I won't. I don't like to hurt people's feelings."

"I'm very glad. Why did you want to know?"

He shrugged elaborately. "Aurore was giving money to this thing called a halfway house for runners which is like this bunch of people who want to help Merrow who've run away live in the city and Daddy had a fit that Aurore was making a donation in her own name. So Aurore yelled back at him and said that it was better to put her name on it with a whole list of donors than be mysterious about it. And Daddy said she wasn't going to do it, and Aurore said it was her personal funds not House funds and hadn't he just said that personal funds were nobody else's business when he bought your contract? So Daddy gave in and Aurore won. I just wanted to know what it was about."

"Ah," Caralys said. Any conclusions she might be drawing were tucked neatly away. "Well, I expect it was nothing important. Tell me, Theo, can you teach me to play Tailors and Towers? I haven't played before."

Boral settled back in one of the cushy seats of House Melian's shuttle, carefully fastening the shoulder straps that crossed over his body. It was a big shuttle with about thirty seats, no doubt meant to take passengers to merchant ships in orbit. There was more than enough room for the three of them. Caralys and Bister were sitting in the first row to the left, talking quietly. He'd taken a couch to the right just in front of the screen so that he could watch the takeoff. He'd never taken off on any planet other than Morrigan.

There were a lot of things he'd never done before. Boral leaned his head back against the headrest. The shuttle was now beginning to taxi toward the launch pad, the city of Beira glittering with a million lights in the darkness of Full Night. On Morrigan it was always full night. Somehow this way the city looked less alien. And everything here was alien except the reality of it—that little girl was going to lose her brother, and that wasn't right. You knew when you were born to a tower as he was, the son of an electromancer mother, that people would move in and out of your life whenever somebody somewhere decided they would. You didn't have a say about who your brothers and sisters were or for how long.

He'd been at Sea Easting his entire life. Eighteen other kids had been and gone. Most had been older, sent for a few years and then reassigned as adults. One of the best things about the battle against the Calpurnians had been seeing them again, or at least hearing a bunch of them on the comm, all the brothers and sisters he'd had and lost. But things were changing. Now he'd see them again. His father said so. He'd seen them. Boral would too, and soon, but right now Boral had the privilege of being one of the first electromancers allowed off Morrigan in a hundred years, so he'd better not screw up.

And here he was, off doing his own thing and running his own mission. If it made a mess, the Warlady would discipline him. No, that wasn't even the worst thing. The worst thing would be the disappointment on his father's face, saying he expected better of Boral. So somehow this had to come out right. He glanced over at Caralys and Bister. "What's the plan?" he asked. "Give me the rundown."

Bister looked like that was a good question. "So we dock with *Liberty*, and then what?"

"I speak with Cassian and Junia," Caralys said. "I tell them we're complying with their demands. I ask to see Theo while they're unloading the currency, which is all completely legitimate. The other passengers and crew from *Light Dancer* come aboard this shuttle. I follow. I ask if the two of you can stay with Theo, which is perfectly reasonable if the staff that was with him on *Light Dancer* is leaving. It's replacing two staffers with two other staffers. The shuttle leaves. Then the two of you break Theo out." She frowned. "It's that part I'm a little sketchy on."

"We can handle it," Bister said. "We've just got to be flexible. We'll see the opportunity and take it." Caralys nodded. "Boral's good at what he does. Have you been on a Calpurnian warship before, Boral?"

"Not a Calpurnian, no," Boral said. "I've been on Morriganian warships. And I've fought Calpurnian warships, but from outside."

"Believe me, that's the best place to see them from," Bister said with the ghost of a smile.

The Calpurnian ship sure looked big on the screen. Boral felt his heart beat faster. He made himself stop and look at it the way he would from *Spider*, the way he had when they'd been facing them inside the Belt, trying to intercept. *Liberty* wasn't the biggest he'd ever seen. It was a frigate, not a ship of the line. He counted six missile tubes, four 500 launchers around the middle, plus two 250s, mounted forward and aft. That wasn't terrible. He'd seen worse. As they came in on approach to the dorsal airlock, he could see the scars of repaired battle damage. At Morrigan? Had he inflicted some of that damage? Had his brothers and sisters? Boral felt a kind of pride swell in him. Yeah. They'd done this. He could do this. It was just that this time he had to be sneaky.

The docking protocol went smoothly, at least as far as he could tell. Bister was listening carefully to the hull sounds, despite the crew compartment being separated from the passenger cabin. Caralys seemed unconcerned, which she did about a lot of things that would have had him sweating—but maybe it was a pose, like *Spider*'s captain's sense of humor or Master Castal-Edo's fancy clothes. Boral leaned back casually in his seat like he did this all the time.

"Well," Bister said. "Showtime."

Caralys unstrapped and got to her feet, her chin going up and her back straight, like she was playing a queen in one of Abi's plays. She gathered her half-cloak around her left arm. "Then let's go."

Boral followed her out through the airlock, blinking in the lights as they came through the hatch onto the Calpurnian ship. They had twelve Marines waiting and a junior officer, which Boral felt was really overkill for three people, given that each Marine was armed with an energy flail.

"House Melian," the junior officer said with a bow of his head.

"Worthy officer," Caralys said with the same inclination. "I am Caralys Sardai i Melian. These are my retainers."

"I'm sorry, ma'am, but I must scan you for weapons." He didn't look much older than Boral himself, Boral thought. He'd be embarrassed to scan Caralys, and it wouldn't be helped by her holding her arms out to the sides, the transparent panels showing her side and her upper leg. There was something uncomfortable about it, though she submitted to the scan docilely. Of course she was unarmed.

Boral stood perfectly still while he was scanned, looking at the floor between the officer's feet. He felt the electrical pulse wash over him. *Weapons*, he thought, *ha! Space-boy, I'm a weapon.* Bister was next, looking old and tired and like she wasn't worth bothering with. He wondered how she did that.

"Come this way, please." Six Marines fell in ahead of them and six behind, the officer walking just ahead of Caralys, with Bister and Boral following after. "The Altissimus Cassian would like to speak with you."

"And I would like to speak with him," Caralys replied.

They were ushered into what must be the officers' mess, with a long, polished table and chairs bolted to the floor for jump. There was a screen at one end, but it showed only an orbital view of Menaechmi below, the Cities of the Coast like a chain of lights against the darkness of ocean and desert. There were two Calpurnian officers present, one a man with closely cropped hair and a scar on his face. He wore a red shipsuit, the insignia of a Grand Admiral, which to Boral seemed a bit out of place on a frigate. The other was a woman perhaps Bister's age in a plain white shipsuit, her hair cut in a wedge at her shoulders.

With a smooth movement, Caralys went to her knees, her

arms outstretched at waist level. "Altissimi," she said, her eyes cast down. "Thank you for the very great honor of speaking with you on behalf of House Melian."

"And the city of Beira," the woman in white said sharply.

"And the city of Beira, of course," Caralys replied. She didn't move. The man shifted from foot to foot, as it was hard to address her at his knees. And she'd completely disarmed any attempt to shame her by kneeling first of her own free will, Boral thought. "I have brought the full amount of the currency that you and the Guardian agreed upon. It is being unloaded from my shuttle now."

"And the recruits?" the man demanded. "Where are they?"

"It will take some time to secure them," Caralys said. "We have been celebrating a holy day, and it was not an opportune moment to draft young people from their families. To do so on a day set aside for the gods would cause great displeasure in the city." She did not raise her eyes.

"I don't care if it causes displeasure," said the man, who was presumably Cassian though he hadn't bothered to introduce himself. "We need those recruits now. We don't have a lot of time."

The woman in white moved. "It's more to the point to ask when we may expect the first cohort. How many hours will it take you to assemble fifty volunteers? That's not much."

"Within a day, I believe," Caralys said.

"One of your days or ours?" the man snapped. "Junia, we can't sit here forever. Either they start delivering, or we start 'recruiting' ourselves."

"One of yours," Caralys said. Surely her legs should shake, kneeling so long, but she was steady as a stone. "And noble Altissimus, we have begun delivering. The entirety of the currency you requested is now aboard your ship." She looked up, her glance taking in him and the woman both. "I therefore rely upon your honor to let me meet with Theo Melian so that I may assure his father of his health and well-being."

Junia nodded. "Yes, that is what we agreed. The crew and passengers of your ship are on their way to your shuttle. I will have you taken to the boy. I assure you he is in good health."

"Thank you, noble Altissima," Caralys said. She looked up from under her long eyelashes. "Your generosity is a model to all."

"You can get up then," Junia said. "Subaltern, take them to the guest quarters to see the boy."

Caralys got gracefully to her feet. "I am forever in your debt, Altissimi." She followed the junior officer out, Boral and Bister scrambling after.

Bister leaned close to Boral. "And that, son, is how you top from the bottom."

They were ushered into the boy's cabin. "Cara!" Boral hadn't even gotten though the door before the kid threw himself on Caralys and she caught him tight.

"I've been so worried about you," she said as the door closed behind them, the Calpurnian guards staying in the corridor. "Theo, have they hurt you?" She took his face in both hands, searching it.

"No. I promise. No." Still on the wrong side of a growth spurt, Boral thought, the kind of twelve that looks ten, slight and childlike and too young for his age. Boral acutely remembered that phase himself, wondering if he was ever going to grow, while Master Castal-Edo had assured him that it was just a matter of time. The next half-year he'd grown seven centimeters and four the half-year after. At sixteen he'd been as tall as his father himself, and he was a tall man. Boral had topped him last year and was still getting used to his height.

Theo was on the short side. He had absolutely straight dark hair that was neatly combed halfway down his back and long eyelashes. He wore black leggings and a tunic in shades of blue, woven and knitted patches put together in an elaborate pattern. Boral supposed they weren't intended to be playclothes. He'd had all playclothes at that age. His father said he didn't need court dress until he was older and it was too expensive to replace each year. Which was true since he hadn't gone to Holyrood until he was nineteen. Theo probably needed court dress.

"Are you sure?" Caralys was still looking into his face, her arm tight around him.

"Yes, Cara!" Theo gave her another squeeze. "You worry too much. I'm fine. But nobody will tell me anything about what's going on. I never see anybody except Ilin bringing me food. But she doesn't know what's going on either. What happened? What's Daddy doing?"

Bister looked at Boral meaningfully.

"Your father is negotiating for your freedom," Caralys said. "And we have just brought currency to ransom the passengers and crew of *Light Dancer*."

Boral faded back against the wall by the door, standing with his back to the wall and putting one hand against it by his leg. He closed his eyes. There. There was the familiar web of wires and fibers that made up the interior of a starship's walls, the hundreds of connections and nodes that were the circulatory system of the ship, electricity flowing like blood. It was easy to touch it. It was easy to perceive, to start tracing each bright spark. There, closest, were the door controls that held it locked. He let that be for now, noting its position. He followed the running current, yes, that. There was a node, the devices attached to it. One tiny spark, one tiny disconnection, leaving the other alone.

Boral opened his eyes. "You can talk now," he said. "I've blown out the microphone, but we're still on camera. It's at this end, just over my left shoulder, so keep your back to it if you're saying something important or walk down to this end of the room and stand behind where I'm standing."

Bister grinned. "Great job."

"What?" Theo looked baffled.

"We'll explain later," Caralys said. "Just do as he says." She looked impressed. "I don't know how long they'll let me visit with you. I promise, Theo, there is a plan to rescue you. This is Boral and Bister. They'll be staying with you as your attendants."

Theo looked from one to the other. "I don't remember seeing you before."

"You haven't," Caralys said. "But pretend you have. They're special agents here on your father's orders." Which was stretching the truth a little, Boral thought. Or maybe not much. He had no idea what Helios Melian knew or directed. Everything about him was confusing.

"All right," Theo said. "What am I supposed to do?"

"Just follow directions and stick with us when the time comes," Bister began.

The door opened. Boral stepped away from the wall as two Marines with energy pikes came in flanking the Altissimus Cassian. Erg, Boral thought. The microphone had given them away, or they'd decided to cut the visit short.

Caralys stepped in front of Theo. "Altissimus, I am surprised! I've barely had a chance to speak with Theo. May I have more time?"

Cassian smirked. "You may. I've discovered that you are not simply an employee of House Melian, but the Guardian's mistress. As we speak, the shuttle is departing with your crew and the other passengers from Light Dancer, but you will not be accompanying it. Two hostages are better than one."

"That was not our agreement," Caralys said, her voice low and for once not sweet.

"I am altering our agreement," Cassian replied. "You and the boy will be released when we have your recruits aboard this ship, and no sooner. I expect the Guardian will be motivated."

"Yes, I expect so." Caralys raised her chin. "Very well. We will wait."

"You have no other choice." He stepped backwards through the door, the guards following. It closed and the lock clicked shut.

"That bastard," Caralys said, pacing across the room.

"He lied." Bister shrugged. "So now we have his measure. Your crew and passengers are safe, and the next move is Helios Melian's."

"He didn't pay any attention to us," Boral said.

"As far as it goes, our mission is the same," Bister said. "Boral and I have to get both you and Theo out instead of just Theo. Not much difference."

"The two Marines are outside in the hallway," Boral said. "I can feel the battery packs on their pikes."

"You could overload them?"

Boral nodded. "Yeah, but not quietly. They'd get off an alarm. We'd have half the ship down on us before we got to the end of the hall."

"Then we wait," Bister said. "Gets pretty boring, standing there guarding nothing."

"I have my luggage and my handheld," Theo volunteered. "They didn't take that away but there's no wired connection in here. There's a sanitary facility in that cupboard. And a bunk bed." He gestured with his chin. "They do bring food."

"We're patient," Boral said. "It's all positive. We just wait for an opening."

"Helios will give us one," Caralys said. "I have no idea what."

Chapter Eight

Caralys sat down on one end of the bunk bed. Frankly her shoes were painful. They weren't meant for this much standing. Theo was playing some game on his handheld with Boral, who either had played the game himself or was a very good sport. Caralys smiled. Theo was a social child. Being alone for so many hours had been difficult for him.

Bister sat down on the other end of the bunk. Her eyes didn't move toward the camera, but angled so that her face was away from it, blocking Caralys's head from it at the same time. "How long do you think?"

"A while." Caralys massaged her ankle. It had swollen around the strap. "Helios has to get home after the rite, read my notes, and then make his move. More currency? Some kind of ruse? I don't know."

"You know him very well, though." Bister leaned back against the wall. "How long have you been together?"

"Nearly five years." She gave up and simply took her shoe off. They'd have enough warning of whatever for her to put it back on, surely. "He bought out my indenture."

"I thought you were from a rich family? How did that work?"

Caralys sighed. "Menaechmi is complicated. I'm from an old House, yes, but blood isn't currency. My House didn't have a great deal of currency, and I was not mainline family. I'm from a cadet line. I had to make my own way in the world, so I started training as a gaura. I completed my training at nineteen and worked for a respectable gambling club as a dancer and hostess." She glanced over at Bister, expecting censure and seeing none. Some offworlders were very judgmental, for all that they flooded to every pleasure palace as tourists. "I was in the shows as a soloist—I was quite good, actually."

"I had a relationship with a dancer once," Bister said. "It's demanding work."

"It is. And physically difficult." Caralys shrugged. "I'd been doing it four years when I broke my foot." She flexed her toes, each nail painted the exact shade of her dress. "I couldn't dance for months, so they let me go. I ran out of money and had to take an indenture."

Bister nodded. "Shit happens, huh? I take it the terms sucked."

"Yes," Caralys said. "I didn't have a lot of options, so I took the contract even though the terms were bad. No salary, just tips. Everything purchased for my use with House money belonged to the House, down to shoes and lingerie. No sex with anyone outside the mainline family except with their express permission. No pregnancy, with me fully responsible for preventing or ending the same. Seven years, with full consent given to anything requested by any of the mainline family, barring actions that would cause me potential physical injury or death."

"So you gave consent in writing to anything they wanted?"

"Anything that wouldn't require medical attention, yes." Caralys looked over at Theo, who seemed to be explaining some complex bit of game strategy to Boral. "I told you it was a bad contract. But it was better than the alternatives. I had no money and no family to turn to and I couldn't work as a dancer. And pretty faces are cheap, as I'm sure you know."

"I do," Bister said. "I've done all kinds of work myself. I got passage from Eresh to Menaechmi when I was about sixteen and discovered pretty quickly that I wasn't the only cute kid in Ashkela." She crossed her legs. "That was the first time I was here. How'd you get from there to being Helios Melian's gaura? I heard he bought out your contract?"

Caralys nodded. "I met him at a party my employers gave. Literally fifteen minutes' conversation. I asked him to buy out my indenture. I have no idea why—it was a ridiculous thing to ask and I'd just met him. I suppose I thought that the worst thing that would happen is that he would take it as a joke." She shook her head. "The last thing I expected was to be awakened the next twilight to hear that House Melian's vehicle was waiting for me and that my indenture had been transferred in full with all terms to Helios Melian. I nearly passed out!"

"I would have too," Bister said. "But maybe he liked it that you seized the moment. Lucky." She grinned. "I always say that the gods help those who help themselves."

"I am very lucky," Caralys said. "And I know it. That's why I'm working with Valeri, who you saw at the temple, and a couple of others, to build a refuge for streetwalkers. The ones who are in the Guild are protected by Guild law and are relatively safe, but the ones who are just part-timers, no formal training, no membership—they have no protection at all. That's the lowest level of personal services."

"And the top level?" Bister asked.

"The Adepts, of course. The Adepts of the Theon in Ashkela, dedicated to the Lord of the Dance, are known throughout the Nine Worlds." Caralys leaned back against the wall beside Bister. "You have to be very, very good to be an Adept. I don't have what it takes. My range is too limited."

"Your range?"

Caralys thought about how best to put it. "You have to have a deep empathy, something that lets you build a bond with a client. And you have to be emotionally and physically responsive to at least four out of five genders with a genuine attraction and connection."

"And you're not?" Bister asked curiously.

"I like hapaloi, dissones and xalepiae to a certain extent. I've never been attracted to hapaliae, and I generally find xalepoi distasteful. Generally." There was a notable exception, but that had been under extraordinary circumstances. "And you?"

Bister grinned. "Well, obviously I find hapaliae attractive, and dissones. I suppose I default to xalepoi more often than not. I like them all, actually."

"That's one thing they look for in an Adept," Caralys said. "The full range is pretty uncommon."

Bister shrugged. "I heard about applying when I was in Ashkela, but I can't dance and I can't sing and I was never that good looking. I wouldn't make an Adept. But it would be something to spend a Full Night with one. That's the stuff fantasies are made of." She glanced sideways at Caralys. "Have you ever done it?"

Caralys looked over to the boys, still engrossed in their game. "Once. It was a gift to me from Helios on my birthday after we'd been together a year." Theo was paying them absolutely no attention. "It is an extraordinary experience."

Bister whistled. "That's quite a present."

"There is an interview first. A senior Adept discusses with you exactly what you want to experience and why. It is the height of my art." She glanced at Bister, who was listening attentively. "There are eight pavilions: Ocean, Forest, Durance," she ticked them off on her fingers. "Celestial, Infernal, Pastoral, Orbital, and Palatial. Each lends itself to different expressions of sacred sexuality. And it is sacred. Bister, I cannot even begin to explain what it's like."

"It sounds incredible," Bister said quietly. "I wish I could do that. I have so many questions and so few answers."

"I know that I found answers there," Caralys said.

"Who did you pick and which pavilion?"

Caralys shook her head, still smiling. "That's a question you don't ask. It's private."

"I see," Bister said. "I'm sorry."

"I'm not offended. But if you ever have the chance to do it, you will understand why."

She'd sat in the quiet conversation nook with a woman old enough to be her mother, suddenly with no idea what she might want or why. In the flyer from Beira she'd considered so many attractive possibilities—luxury and pampering, sweet indulgence, to have no one to please but herself, to have someone devoted to pleasing her with no strings attached, no need to wonder if her desires were appropriate to her persona. She could enjoy a massage and then leisurely pleasure without considering someone else's needs. She would not be a demanding client. And now she sat in a soft taupe chair, carefully neutral in a carefully neutral, comfortable room, unable to think of anything.

"Orbital," she said. Orbital was the set that resembled a derelict space station, dirty and run down, with metal floors and thin cots, bars and pipes and flickering florescent lights. It was everything she'd always hated. There was no refinement, no beauty or comfort. It was nasty.

The Senior Adept simply nodded, her eyes never leaving Caralys's face. "Of course. And your choice of partner?"

Her voice was hard, harsh, barely her own. "Xalepos," she said. "Young and handsome and bearded, with good muscles. A man who likes a beating."

There was a faint smile on the Senior Adept's face. "I know just the right one."

His name was Adrian. She whipped him until she nearly drew blood with him bound to the floor-to-ceiling pipes, then rode him on the plastic cot, his bruised back and buttocks and legs banging with each movement. It was savage, angry, ruinous. She was a harridan, a man-eater, cruel and selfish like the Lady of the Void who drinks men's blood poured into the darkness between the stars.

Afterwards, Caralys lay against the wall and he pulled a soft white blanket over them both. "Well," Adrian said cheerfully, "that was a good run. I won't be able to sit down tomorrow."

She looked at him incredulously, guilt curling around in her stomach. "You're not upset?"

Adrian shrugged. "No. Why would I be?" He settled down beside her, hairy chest, dark beard and beautiful green eyes. Every inch of him was physical perfection, a dancer's body with strong arms. He was probably her age to the year. "This is what I like. And it's not often I have someone so beautiful and easy to please."

"That was easy?" For her it would have been something best forgotten, if it ever could be.

"For me," he said. He put his arm around her and she nestled in gratefully. It was suddenly cold. The blanket and Adrian were warm. "Besides," he said with a cocky grin, "Helios Melian's gaura. I've seen you on the nets. Always dressed in the latest and looking sweeter than honey candy." He snugged the blanket closer. "So you're spice as well as sweetness."

Caralys shook her head. "No. Not really."

"Your lover doesn't like this?"

The very idea was ludicrous. "Helios? No, never. He doesn't like pain, neither to receive nor give. Passion, yes. But pain? He doesn't like to see anyone hurt." Adrian's eyebrows rose, and she rushed on. "I mean, he gets angry. Who doesn't? He yells, but not at me because it makes me cry. He only yells at people who yell back. It's a family of yellers. They have big emotions and shout at each other. But he knows that it scares me, so he never yells at me. And he can be cuttingly sarcastic. But he's never cruel. He doesn't take pleasure in hurting people."

Adrian shook his head. "That's not what I expected."

"I took pleasure in hurting you." The guilt rose again, sick and hot at once.

He had an insouciant smile. "And I took pleasure in being hurt. We're all different. You're so sweet."

"Perfect hapalia," Caralys said. "Fragile as a night-blooming flower. Delicate and easily bruised by rudeness. Tender and yielding."

"Are you?"

She lay back on his arm. "Maybe. Usually." Caught still in the intensity, there was a kind of clarity. "I certainly like tenderness," she said slowly. "And I appreciate that he's never asked me to do something I didn't want to do, not once, when he could have anything he wants. He's easy to please, at least for me. He wants passion and kindness and just a dirty edge of the forbidden, but nothing too dark. He likes to give. I think he enjoys giving as much as having."

"Maybe he's the one who should have been an Adept," Adrian observed.

"Maybe so." She stopped, thinking. "Sometimes there's something so old in his eyes. A whisper of the Golden Lady and her Husband. He wears it like a cloak, gracefully, almost guilelessly." She looked at Adrian. "You know what I mean."

"I do." There was a touch of the strange in him for a moment. "But the Lord of the Dance is a law unto himself."

"And the Lord of the Dance has a dark side," Caralys said. "Just like the Golden Lady has. Helios belongs to Beira and to Her. And yes, he's self-indulgent and he's vain and I'm sure he has a great many flaws. But cruelty's not one. No one has ever been kinder to me."

"It sounds like you love him," Adrian observed.

She turned her face, looking up at the grid of the metal ceiling above her head, artfully rusted. "I do. And I would never say it. You don't fall in love with a client."

"Why not? You don't have our restrictions." Adrian reached

for one of the artificially tattered pillows and put it beneath his head. "Does he love you?"

"Probably. At least he's infatuated with me. I absolutely believe he's infatuated with me. I live in his suite. He indulges my whims and I join him at openings and official engagements and dinners in the playroom with his children." She blinked at the ceiling. "But what happens when he gets tired of me? I'm not a changeable person. I might find someone else, but I would never stop loving him. If he tires of me, he'll release me from the contract with a generous settlement and I will have the money and friends to do something else in comfort. But I won't have him. No one really has him except the Lady."

"Everything changes," Adrian said, that same shadow in his eyes. "In the natural course of time, you will outlive him by many years."

"I know," Caralys said quietly, "so I cherish every day."

Adrian smiled, the shadow gone. "Do you find him attractive?"

Caralys ducked her head, feeling a genuine hapalia blush rise. "Yes. Terribly. And the sex is good. Better than good. Wonderful. I mean, he has a co-sleeping kink, but so do I. We're well-matched."

He looked like he was about to laugh. "So your problem is that you're in love with a man who is in love with you, who you live with, who happens to be handsome, rich, generous and good in bed?"

"When you put it that way…." She managed kind of a breathless giggle. "It does sound absurd, doesn't it?" Adrian shrugged. "I just wonder—"

"Wonder what?"

"If I were more honest, what would happen? I mean, I am hapalia, but sometimes it gets exhausting, to be perfect and soft all the time. What would happen if I did something off? When he asks what I want to drink, if I didn't burble and say something sweet and fruity, but said fermented succulent on ice? What would happen if I looked unkempt?"

"What do you think would happen?" Adrian asked.

"I think he'd raise an eyebrow and get my drink," Caralys said. "And I don't expect he'd say anything, unless it was for some official event."

"I put it to you that if you want his heart, you have to bet yours," Adrian said. "Your real self, not perfect hapalia, but your wonderful, imperfect self. The Golden Lady loves a gambler. Maybe it's time for you to put a bigger bet on the table."

Caralys nodded slowly. "And see how the cards come up." She took a deep breath. "Games of money, games of power."

Adrian's eyes were gentle. "You have power. Right now, you have more power than half of Beira. What are you going to do with your power?" He stretched against her. "You don't have to use power to hurt people just because some people hurt you. You can choose what to do with it."

A connection clicked. "Helios has power and he's the most restrained person I know. He's careful with me and with everything he touches." A memory fit into place. "House Melian isn't an old House. A while ago I bought him several antique robes from a very discreet dealer I know who handles such things, hand-painted robes eighty to a hundred years old, vintage silk painted by a master who died in the war. Old Houses sell things like that sometimes. First you sell the robes, then the furniture and then the children. Anyway, House Melian doesn't have anything like that. They didn't have money eighty years ago. So I bought several when they became available, wearable works of art really. He is so careful with them. You'd think they were porcelain or a newborn baby."

"And so beautiful things are treated as they should be," Adrian said. "Power. Art. Which of you is which?"

She laughed. That was the question and the answer at the same time. "Both. We are each both. He is as much of an artist as I am."

"And you are as much of a ruler?"

Caralys blew out a long breath. "Oh, that's the scary thought." His brows twitched. "You've given me a lot to think about."

"I am supposed to," Adrian said.

She returned to Beira in Greater Morning, the sun making flashing patterns on the waves as the flyer came in over the sea, the Old Man sleeping beneath its puff of cloud, the city spread at its feet in all its decadence and glory. Tears stung her eyes.

A Melian trundle took her home. Yes, home, and she hurried up the lift and through the outer rooms to find Helios in the study, frowning over columns of figures on one screen and tariff tallies on the other. "Cara!" he said, and she threw herself on him, pushing him back on the pillows and kissing him as if it had been ten Days.

"Don't talk," she said. "Love me."

It was quite some time later that they lay tangled on the couch, the first white clouds beginning to form far out to sea. She opened her left hand against his chest, smooth and waxed as always. Everything seemed nearer and more precious and dear.

"I take it you enjoyed your Full Night?" Helios asked.

"Very much." She could practically hear him trying not to ask. Curiosity was killing him, but he wouldn't pry. "Orbital," she said. "And xalepos." His face changed just a little. "I beat him black and blue."

"Cara." He curved his hand around her shoulder. "I...."

"It was cathartic. Not something I'd want to do often." She caressed his chest, warm and nude and vulnerable. "I prefer hapaloi. And I prefer you." There was something she should share. "The Adept asked me if my problem was really that I was in love with a man who loved me and was handsome, rich, generous and good in bed." She watched. She watched to see how his expression would change.

It did. His eyes didn't leave hers. "Cara."

"Because I do. And that's simply how it is." And there was the kiss, passionate enough to make her head spin. She held onto him as though he might somehow be pulled away in a rip current.

His eyes were still closed when they parted. "I love you too, and you'll have to decide if that's a terrible misfortune."

"Why would it be?"

He looked away, at the patterns the sea reflection made on the ceiling. "There are quite a few things you may not like."

"I'll take the risk," Caralys said. She put her hand to the side of his face, turning it back to her. "And you may find that there are things you don't like about me either, if I'm not trying so hard to be the perfect hapalia gaura."

His mouth twitched in a smile. "I'll double and let it ride."

Boral nearly fell asleep on the floor. It had been hours. A guard had been in with a tray and they'd eaten. Theo was sleeping on the bed. Bister leaned up against the wall, her eyes closed. And Caralys had finally settled down leaning against the bunk beside Theo's head. Apparently sharing the bunk was some kind of taboo even though he thought of her as a mother.

Boral took the floor. The floor was actually nice. He could feel all the cables running beneath the deck, the ventilation system that served the deck below, and one of the main trunk lines carrying the fiber information cables aft was just a few feet away. If the floor was transparent to you, it was like lying in a tree made of light.

He traced the cables, half in dreams. There was a lifecraft cluster just aft, a useful thing to know. And there were the cables to the aft missile launcher, also useful. It was a very pretty tree. He dozed, and so he was surprised when the door opened.

Four Marines stepped in with a young officer. He cleared his throat. "I'm sorry to disturb your rest, but the Altissimi require your presence. Pack up your things."

"Why?" Theo asked, sitting up on the bed.

"You're being exchanged," the young officer said.

Caralys and Bister traded a look. "For what?" Caralys asked.

"I'm sorry, ma'am. I'm not party to the terms."

"Of course." Caralys got to her feet. "Theo, get your handheld."

Boral stood up, trying to be as inconspicuous as possible. He was just this guy. He was nobody in particular. He felt the prickle of the energy flail on the officer's belt, like it was just itching for his hand. There was a lot of ambient around, all the ship's systems. If he needed it, it was there.

They followed the officer through the ship, Boral bringing up the rear with two Marines behind him, deep into the belly of the ship. *The command center*, Boral thought. *That's what you put inboard, where it's least likely to take a hit.* Doors swished open ahead of them. He was right. It was the command center, carpeted in scarlet with three large screens around the front of the room, eight acceleration couches arranged in a semi-circle. Used to the cramped command center on *Spider*, it seemed spacious, but then *Liberty* was a frigate.

Altissimus Cassian turned, his Grand Admiral's insignia still seeming incongruous given that he seemed to command one ship. "You will be exchanged," he said without preliminaries. "Theo Melian and Caralys Sardai i Melian will return to Menaechmi aboard a Menaechman shuttle."

"Your pardon, gracious Altissimus," Caralys said. "But what are we being exchanged for?"

"I'm glad you ask," Cassian began.

The door behind them opened again. Four more Marines flanked Helios Melian.

Boral was glad he wasn't looking at Caralys. She made some sound that was almost a moan.

Helios Melian greeted Cassian with a smile. "Altissimus. It's a pleasure." He wore a Melian blue raw silk tunic that came to his knees, buttoned up the front with tiny gold buttons. Beneath it his lower legs were covered in matching silk pants, tight and buttoned up the back of the ankles. A long silk vest went all the way to the floor, every inch of it embellished with golden honeybees in a fantastic jungle of flowers of gold and crystal beads. The sleeves of the tunic matched, vines twining around his wrists, one whimsical honeybee flying up his arm.

Theo ran to him. "Daddy!" He plastered himself against his father's chest. "I knew you'd straighten everything out."

"Indeed he has, young man," Cassian said. "He has exchanged himself for you. And the courtesan, of course."

Theo took a step back, still with his father's arms around him, looking up. Of course he was smart enough to see the problem, Boral thought. Trading him for Master Castal-Edo would be a huge tactical mistake. On the other hand, it was a deal his father would be likely to make, if the Warlady didn't stop him. Boral cast a glance at Bister. She stood scrupulously silent, as though she were trying to size up the changing situation.

"So," Cassian said. "You will be our guest until the promised recruits arrive."

"Of course," Helios Melian said. His eyes met Caralys's over Theo's head. She was pale and still, her face frozen.

"You will return to Beira on the shuttle that the Guardian arrived on," Cassian said. "Off you go."

"Daddy…" Theo began.

"Go on, Theo," Helios said, bending down and kissing him hard. "It will be all right." He looked at Bister. "Take him to the shuttle."

Bister nodded. Well, thought Boral, what else could she do, in her House Melian blues? Getting the child out was her mission. They headed toward the door, flanked by the Marine escort.

"Wait!" Caralys said, turning to Cassian. "Would you leave him without even a bodyservant? The boy stays." Boral stopped in his tracks.

Cassian seemed to be relishing the moment. "Why not?" He smiled jovially. "Guardian, your servant may stay. Take the others to the shuttle."

Boral nodded, glancing at Helios Melian, wondering what he knew. Caralys had said she would be leaving him notes, but he had no idea what she'd said or if Melian had read them. They were out the door now. It closed behind Caralys. Boral went to stand a few respectful paces behind Helios Melian, as an apprentice would with a master at home, folding his hands deferentially.

"Now we shall confer," Cassian said. "Face to face and man to man." He seemed to take up a great deal of room, as though he made himself as large as possible, tough and manly. Next to him the Guardian looked every bit the effete ruler of a client state. The Warlady didn't need tricks like that, Boral thought. She expected you to respect her on her own merits, and Khreesos help anyone who didn't. "You will arrange for the first fifty recruits to be delivered in ten hours. I don't care if you sweep up the secondary schools. I will have fifty young people between eighteen and twenty-four on this ship in ten hours."

"We will do our best to comply, of course," the Guardian said. "It's simply a difficult situation. We don't have a legal mechanism for compelling military service."

"Let me make this clear,' Cassian said. "I don't care whether you have a legal mechanism or not. Find one."

"The government of Beira…" the Guardian began.

"The government of Beira had better understand that Calpurnia is tired of excuses. You can come up with recruits if you are motivated to do so."

"It will take time, Altissimus," the Guardian said placatingly. He looked sincere and troubled. "Of course I am sensible of your position and your needs. It's just that this is a matter of logistics. We have every respect for your wishes and are eager to grant them."

"I don't believe the government of Beira understands the gravity of their situation. You are a city-state of six million. We are an empire of eight billion. You will cooperate, willingly or unwillingly. It will be much simpler for you if you do so willingly."

"Altissimus," the Guardian said, spreading his hands. "We are attempting to cooperate in every way. I am fully aware that conflict with Calpurnia would be disastrous. It's just that what you ask is beyond my humble ability to provide. I am not a planetary ruler as you yourself are. I do not have great powers at my command. If this is taking longer than you wish, you have my apologies. I am endeavoring to provide everything you desire as quickly as possible."

Cassian paced a few steps, then stopped and looked back at him. "Why do I feel like you're stalling, Melian?"

"I assure you I am not," the Guardian said with a bow.

One of the officers at a forward console interrupted him. "Admiral, the shuttle has launched."

"Excellent," Cassian said. He put his hands behind his back. "Perhaps we need an example of why cooperation is essential. Lieutenant, clear the forward missile tube. Prepare to fire on the shuttle."

"What?" Melian demanded.

"Perhaps this will motivate you," Cassian said. "You may fire when ready."

A lot of things happened at once. Helios Melian jumped for Cassian with his bare hands, knocking him back against one of the control boards. Two Marines ignited energy pikes, one sparking erratically, as they moved to their Admiral's defense. The weapons officer initiated the launch sequence.

Melian got his hands around Cassian's throat, and then an energy pike hit him in the side, knocking him off as the other Marine touched his pike to his back, Melian's entire body arcing with the charge, his teeth grinding as he screamed.

Boral reached for the missile. *Blessed Khreesos, my range is so short, if it gets going I'll never get it, I can't hit it at ten kilometers....*

Cassian dragged himself up from the board clutching his bruised throat. The Marine hit Melian again.

"Admiral," the weapons officer said, "We have an ignition

problem. The missile failed to launch. We'll have to remove it from the tube manually."

On the screen the shuttle streaked toward Beira, ducking lower into the atmosphere. Boral took a deep breath. If they launched from another tube he'd have to get that too, and he probably could, but two ignition failures was too much to be coincidence. They'd start wondering why it happened.

Two Marines hauled the Guardian to his feet. There was blood at the corner of his mouth, his fists balled though he was shaking from the electrical shocks. He seemed to be having trouble standing.

Cassian smiled. "You see that making trouble is useless. Shall we continue with this demonstration? Clear the dorsal tube."

Void take you, Boral thought. He was going to have to do it again. He focused on the dorsal tube, trying to find the guidance system of the loaded missile.

"Admiral, another ship is coming out of jump!" another officer said. The screen showed it, a ship the size of a frigate sliding into view just outsystem of them. It was sleek and black, bristling with missile tubes, a grinning skull with ivory teeth painted on its side. "It's one of the Ereshan pirates!"

"Ereshan pirates?" Cassian spun around. "What are they doing here?"

The comm crackled. "Hailing the Calpurnian frigate which seems to be loading missiles," a man's voice said. "Is this a hostile act toward us or toward that shuttlecraft?"

Cassian grabbed the comm himself. "Who in the name of the Infernal are you?"

"This is the Ivory Captain," the pirate replied. "And I believe there are hostilities between Calpurnia and Eresh."

CHAPTER NINE

Bister leaned over the shuttle pilot's shoulder and toggled open the comm. "Holla, Tal. Nice to see you! Think you can cover the shuttle until it lands?"

Tal Robber's voice sounded a little amused. "Holla yourself, Bister. Of course we can. Bit off more than you can chew?"

"It's a long story," Bister said. "I take it Jamila gave you the message I sent?"

"She did," Tal said. On the scanner she could see *Ivory Three* angling to take up a position between the shuttle and *Liberty*. "But we're going to have to talk in a little bit. I've got an angry Calpurnian on the other channel. I need to explain to him that he has no authority to order me out of Menaechman space."

Caralys found her voice. "He absolutely does not. You are welcomed by the City of Beira."

"Good to know," Tal said. "Bister, call me when you've landed if you have access to an encrypted channel."

Caralys nodded. "You will," she said.

"I will," Bister said. "Talk to you in a bit." She stopped leaning over the pilot and settled back in her seat in the row behind, a much smaller shuttle than the one they'd used before. Caralys was next to her, Theo in the seat behind.

Caralys turned toward her, taking Bister's hands in hers. Her eyes were wide but her voice was very deliberately even. "What in the world is going on? Where did that ship come from?"

"That's *Ivory Three*," Bister said. "Her captain is Tal Robber, the Ivory Captain. They're from Eresh, and real good friends of mine. I sent a message with Captain Jamila Ravit when she left. I had a feeling they might be helpful."

"Helpful how?"

Bister disengaged her hands from Caralys to put on her seatbelts for landing. "I figured it like this: you have currency but no fleet and a bunch of Calpurnians shaking you down. They have a fleet but not much currency and Tal hates the Calpurnians. It seemed like there might be a deal in this."

"Rent a pirate ship," Caralys said flatly.

"Essentially." Bister looked cheerful.

"Can I go on the pirate ship?" Theo asked.

"No, you may not," Caralys snapped. "Theo, adults need to talk right now."

"Yes, Cara." He was clearly all ears anyway.

"How much?" Caralys asked.

Bister grinned. "You and Tal will have to work that out. But let me say this—he's a fine captain and he killed Altissima Gnea with his own hands. He hates the Calpurnians a lot. And *Ivory Three* is probably a match for *Liberty*."

The shuttle began its final approach, landing chimes sounding. Caralys sat back in her seat. "Then I am eager to talk with him," she said. "*Liberty* cleared a missile tube and didn't fire," she said thoughtfully. "Perhaps they were threatening the Guardian?"

"Or they meant to fire and Boral fixed it," Bister said.

"He can do that?"

Bister nodded. "So he said. I've never seen such a thing, but he can glitch electronics at close range. The forward tube isn't far from the command center."

Caralys took a deep breath, squaring her shoulders. "Our first stop is House Melian's port offices. We can open a secure channel to *Ivory Three* from there. And then we start trying to make a deal that will get the Guardian off the ship and prevent the Calpurnians from making an example of Beira."

"That was smart, keeping Boral on the ship," Bister said.

"I hope so," Caralys said.

"Get them out of my command center!" Cassian said, gesturing at the Guardian and Boral. "I'll deal with them later." He seemed completely occupied shouting at the pirate captain, who kept saying over and over again that he had every right to be in Menaechman space with what seemed like an air of infuriating amusement in his voice. Junia had just joined Cassian in the command center; maybe she'd calm him down.

The Marines took Boral and the Guardian back to the cabin Boral had been in before with Theo. They went out and locked the door. Helios Melian sat down heavily on the bunk. "Maybe you should lie down," Boral said. "It's fine."

"Nothing in this situation is fine," Melian snapped. He looked ill.

Well, that made sense. "I think you're probably having some heart arrhythmia from the energy pike," Boral said. "That happens. I can fix it." Melian looked at him like he was crazy. Then he glanced around the walls meaningfully. "I already fried the microphone," Boral said. "And if I keep my back to the camera and stay between you and it, we can talk freely. So maybe you should lie down and let me see what I can do."

Melian must have felt rotten, because he lay back where Theo had slept and let Boral take his left hand between his. He could feel his pulse in his wrist—yeah, just a little off from the amount of current that had hit him with the pike. A tiny push would fix that, getting everything working in the right rhythm again. He'd learned this kind of fine work two years ago, and while it wasn't his forte, he could manage something simple. After all, hearts wanted the right rhythm. He closed his eyes, feeling for the minute signals, just like syncing with another electromancer, only matching so that he could mirror the right rhythm off his own heart. This, his father had said, was why electromancers were so feared. Of course, he said that about nearly everything. There. That was the pattern. Boral opened his eyes, letting go of Melian's hand. "How's that?"

He nodded, then cautiously sat up. "Better," he said. He touched his neck. "Better." Then he focused on Boral. "Who are you?"

"Boral. Boral Hailu-Savarin." That didn't seem to elicit any recognition. "I'm an electromancer."

"You're what?"

Boral sat down on the end of the bunk, making sure that his body blocked Melian's face from the camera. "I'm an electromancer. The electromancer from the Morriganian Scout Ship *Spider*."

Melian looked like he was adding things up without half the numbers on the board. "The Morriganians are at war with Calpurnia again?"

"No. At least I hope not. I don't think so. Unless I really mess this up." Boral took a deep breath. "The Calpurnians—they don't know what I am. And if they find out they're going to take me apart. And the Warlady will kill me. I mean, she won't have a chance to kill me because the Calpurnians will experiment on me, so I have to make sure that doesn't happen." The stakes were suddenly looking much higher. "So if they figure it out, they can't take me alive," he finished. If they did, he'd compromise Morrigan's best defense. He'd put everyone he loved at risk. Right now the Calpurnians couldn't counter electromancers. They'd love to have one prisoner to examine. It couldn't be him. Maybe he hadn't thought through this whole thing as well as he should have.

"Well, I suppose we both have a problem," Melian said. He

looked stronger. "Cassian is certainly going to kill me when Beira doesn't do what he wants."

It clicked into place. "You knew that," Boral said. "You did it on purpose. The bull. You promised."

He wasn't being his most articulate self, but Melian's eyebrows rose. "Yes. I swore to give my life for the City."

"I was there," Boral said. "When the bull—I mean, at the rite." And the rest of it. Boral felt the heat rising in his face. He'd watched this man…he wasn't sure what the polite way of putting it was. None of the words that people used in the Fleet seemed right, and making love seemed too insipid. Sleeping together was polite, only nobody was sleeping. "You know," he said.

"I do." Melian looked amused.

"We don't do that on Morrigan," Boral said, then belatedly realized that he'd said that nobody made love. "I mean, not in public."

"I understand Morriganians are modest," Melian said diplomatically.

"Yeah. I guess. I mean, we wear clothes. And things," Boral floundered around. There wasn't any way to explain what he'd felt during the rite, either the one with the sex or the bull killing. It was transporting, amazing, beyond words.

"All that aside," Melian said. "What are you doing here? Why is a Morriganian electromancer wearing my House's colors on board a Calpurnian warship?"

"Didn't Caralys explain all that in her note?" Boral asked. "She said she was going to."

"Her note?"

"She said she was leaving a note on your screen that explained the whole plan."

"On my screen," Melian said. "At House Melian. Where I haven't been. I went straight from the temple to our offices at the starport because the newsnets were covering the release of the crew of *Light Dancer*. I went directly to the starport to talk to them. I haven't been home." He looked up at the ceiling of the little room. "Ah, Caralys. What was the plan?"

"The plan was that we'd come aboard, me and Bister, with her and then she'd leave us with Theo and we'd break him out," Boral said. "Only that went oval when Cassian said he wouldn't release her so we'd have to retool and figure it out."

"Who is Bister?" Melian asked.

"Oh, she's the operator Caralys hired to rescue Theo. She's from Inanna. Caralys promised her if she'd rescue Theo, Beira would repudiate an old treaty."

At that the Guardian nodded gravely. "Ah. Yes. I had that part of the story. It's certainly a fair trade. But how do you come into it?"

"Bister asked me to," Boral said. It sounded stupid that way. "She asked me to help and I said I would because it was right. Kids shouldn't be taken away from their parents and used for political games." Melian dropped his head for a moment. Boral ran on. "I mean, I was born in a tower. I was born at Sea Easting because Hailu is too important a lineage not to pass on, but most of the kids came from somewhere else. They had parents they couldn't see anymore. I was really lucky." He'd never put it that way before, and the guilt that came with it. "My mom was there. I mean, she doesn't make sense most of the time, but she's there. And my dad—my dad is great. He's been there since the day I was born. I'd do anything not to disappoint him."

"Your father is an electromancer?" Melian asked quietly.

Boral nodded. "Master Jauffre Castal-Edo. He's not my progenitor, but he's my father." Melian looked confused. "Not my genetic father but he raised me since I was a baby. He's so proud that I joined *Spider*. You know what the last thing he said to me was? He said, 'Go have some experiences. And have fun.' If I start a war with Calpurnia because I screwed up, he's going to kill me."

Melian looked like he was trying not to laugh. "Yes, parents do tend to get upset when their children start wars by accident."

"So I get Theo. I do."

His face stilled. "How is Theo?"

"Scared," Boral said honestly. "But he's not hurt. He was just really scared. I told him he did great. And he did. It's scary being locked up when you're not used to it." He grinned. "A couple of hours ago we were playing GhoulStalker on his handheld. He's really good at it. Theo said he'd been playing for more than a year, but I just got it. We didn't have screens at the tower, so I didn't start playing until I joined *Spider*. So he kind of kicked my butt. But that's fine."

Melian shook his head, smiling. "I love Theo very much."

"I know," Boral said. "To give your life for his."

Melian looked quickly away. Maybe they weren't supposed to say things like that on Menaechmi. "Yes," he said.

"And Caralys," Boral added.

"And Caralys." He seemed to be looking very intently at the wall.

Boral searched for the diplomatic phrases. "Are you and her… you and Caralys…um, together?" It seemed kind of weird if they were for Caralys to just watch him screwing some other woman and not be upset at all.

"Are we lovers?" Melian said without a trace of embarrassment. "Yes. She is my gaura."

"I don't know what that means," Boral said.

"I hold her indenture," Melian said. "She works for House Melian in a variety of capacities, including clever and dangerous plans." His mouth twitched in a fleeting smile. "But more often she arranges the things that make our lives function: schedules, wardrobes, domestic finances, press access and exposure, transportation, entertainment for business and family functions, and menus and suchlike. She is a charming hostess. And she provides personal services to me."

"Personal services?"

"Sex," Melian said.

"Oh." Boral stared at him. Melian didn't seem at all bothered. "You own her to have sex with you."

"Among other things, as I've said." He looked at Boral thoughtfully. "Doesn't anyone on Morrigan sex someone inside a power differential? I expect if you think, you'll find some examples."

Boral swallowed. "I've been warned my whole life about the Black Guard and the way some of them will take advantage of electromancers. They're supposed to guard us, but there are some of them who harass and molest and rape." He stopped, hitting a wall. His mother waking up screaming. His father standing at the Warlady's side at her Investiture, and then explaining to him very carefully that he and the Warlady had been together since Boral was eight, only it had been too dangerous to talk about. The way he walked behind her chair, leaning over her shoulder to read reports she was getting, his hand on her shoulder, the way she glanced up to see what his reaction was.

Melian was watching him. "Yes?"

"My father," Boral said slowly. "He was the ward of a Guard and they've been together eleven years. He says she's the love of his life. But when they got together, she could do anything to him. She could make him." Boral shook his head. "I don't understand."

"I put it to you that the only people who know what passes between them are those people themselves," Melian said. "And they are the only people who have the right to judge whether this is good or healthy."

Boral looked at the floor. It seemed plain, but beneath it were all the shining branches of electricity, wires and cables like living capillaries. "My mother hated her guards. But my father loves the Warlady."

"The Warlady," Melian said. "Your father knows the Warlady?"

"He stood beside her at her Investiture. He lives in her official suite. He's her companion."

"Ah." Melian looked thoughtful. "The Lady does give us some unexpected cards, doesn't she?"

"What?"

"Just that nothing happens entirely by chance when the gods take a hand." He sat up. He was definitely looking stronger. His hands weren't shaking anymore. "Which brings us to the question of this rescue. Is the pirate ship part of the plan?"

"You've got me there," Boral said. "I don't know anything about it."

"I wonder how it matches up against this ship," Melian mused.

That was an easy question, and Boral went for it gratefully. "*Liberty* mounts four 500s, two dorsal and two ventral. There are a pair of 250s, one forward and one aft. The forward tube is jammed until they can remove the missile that misfired. There's some battle damage on the dorsal surface. I saw it when we arrived."

"The missile," Melian said. For a moment he looked pale. "It was fortunate that it misfired."

Boral shrugged. "That was me. I fried the ignition in the tube. I'm sorry I couldn't get the pikes too, but I can do one thing at a time and stopping the missile was the higher priority."

"You stopped the missile."

"Yes," Boral said. "Electromancer."

Melian closed his eyes and inclined his head formally. "Then I am in your debt. Theo and Caralys..." He halted.

"It's fine," Boral said quickly. The idea of having him in his debt felt uncomfortable. "The pirate ship is mounting at least a pair of 750s, one fore and one aft, and it looked like maybe four 500s too. So I think it's got *Liberty* outgunned and probably has the tonnage on it too, but the pirate ship is a lot older and probably a lot less maneuverable. I didn't see but two sets of maneuvering thrusters."

Melian's brows rose. "And you saw all that in a few moments onscreen?"

"I'm Morriganian Fleet," Boral said proudly. "I served in battle against the Calpurnians at Morrigan a few months ago. I've faced Calpurnian ships of the line, and I know what armament looks like. And how to give a report." He grinned. "They kind of expect you to be able to identify enemy ships."

"Very useful," Melian said. "Which means we have several possibilities open to us. We wait until the pirate ship and this one engage, in which case we are likely to be under fire from an enemy with greater armament."

"I don't like that one," Boral said. "If we're hulled, it won't matter if we're friends or enemies. I might be able to keep a missile from hitting us, but then I'd be giving the Calpurnians the advantage." He shook his head. "I've got a limited range. It was easy to stop the missile launch because it was only about fifty meters to the forward missile tube and Cassian told me exactly what was happening. I could see it. I can't blow up missiles I can't see that are coming at us tens of kilometers away."

"Understood," Melian said. "The second option is that we wait until Caralys follows the directions in the notes I left for her at the port office and tells Cassian that we won't comply with his demands. He probably kills me and jumps outsystem. Which leaves you dead as well or a prisoner."

Boral shook his head. "He won't do that. If she tells him no, he'll fire on the city of Beira."

"That's not how it works. Beira doesn't comply, so he kills the hostage."

Boral met his eyes squarely. "I watched the Calpurnians fire missiles on Holyrood. It's a city of nearly a million people. They would have killed ten thousand people if an apprentice hadn't detonated the missile at the last moment. You think they wouldn't fire on Beira? I've watched them fire on a city and not been able to do anything about it. If they'd do it to us, they'll do it to you."

He watched Melian's face change. "Then we have to escape and stop them," he said.

"Now you're talking," Boral said.

House Melian's port offices were in a low building near the main freight terminal, the façade of the building limned in blue light that was fading fast in the dawn. The Greater Twin was edging above the horizon, ending the holy night. Caralys swept into the office, followed by Bister and Theo, looking around to see who the duty crew was. Fortunately, the one in charge seemed to be Praxi, a middle-aged disson who had been given House membership by Helios's father.

"Gaura," they said with a nod. "We've got about twenty reporters camped out in the lobby. They've already talked to the passengers from *Light Dancer* but I asked the crew not to speak yet. I've sent them home, so who knows if they will or not. I had no authority over the passengers though."

"Of course not." Caralys shook her head. "And they've every right to speak. But we've got to control the message from here on out. Here's the story: Helios Melian is negotiating with the Calpurnians personally."

Their brows rose in their weathered face. "Is that true?"

"Completely," Caralys said. "I left him on the *Liberty* speaking with the Altissimus Cassian. I've brought Theo Melian home." Every word she said was true. It simply wasn't the whole truth.

"And what about that ship from Eresh?"

"That's the next piece," Caralys said. "I need an encrypted channel, use of the office, and some coffee."

"The Guardian left notes for you in the office," Praxi said.

"Good," Caralys said. Maybe Helios had a plan. If so, it would be nice to know what it had been before it got totally messed up.

"What am I supposed to do?" Theo asked.

She put her hands on his shoulders. "I need you to go back to House Melian and take a very important message to Phoebe. And then I need you to get Mia and take her to the storm shelter in the basement and stay there. Phoebe will bring other people in the House down, and you are to obey Aurore and Dian's mother as you would your father until we get back." Theo looked spooked, but he nodded. Under his baby hapalos demeanor he had all of his father's steel, Caralys thought. It just hadn't been tested before now.

"Will you speak to the reporters?" Praxi asked.

"In a while," Caralys said. "I've got other things I have to do first. You can tell them that." Praxi looked like there were ten things they'd rather be doing. "But can you get someone to take Theo to House Melian first?"

"Yes, Gaura."

"We need to talk to Tal," Bister said quietly.

"I know. That's first." Caralys headed toward the office. "Get me the encrypted channel in here first," she called. "And an open line to *Ivory Three*."

The comm set pinged. "Gaura, you have an open line with full encryption," a woman's voice said.

"Thank you, Arys," Caralys said. She took a deep breath and turned on the microphone. "Ivory Captain, this is Gaura Caralys Sardai i Melian of House Melian. Bister is here with me, and I am very pleased to speak with you."

Chapter Ten

Boral leaned back against the wall, thinking. "I can get the door open easy," he said. "But then what? There are two guards with energy pikes in the hall."

"How do you know that?" Melian asked curiously.

"I can feel the battery packs," Boral said. "But I can't take them both at once." He rested his chin on his hands. "There's a lifecraft cluster just aft and overriding the launch protocols is child's play. The problem is the guards."

"I take it you're not a hand-to-hand fighter," Melian said dryly.

"I'm an electromancer," Boral said. "We don't use weapons. We are weapons." Which was not the same as being an old guy, but it wasn't tactful to say that part. "Unfortunately, I can't do the thing my dad does with pulling electricity out of the ambient and throwing it with his hands. I'm better at fine work, like in the body, but I can't throw lightning." Melian's eyebrows went up. "It seems impossible until you see it," Boral said.

"I suppose we could try calling them in and hitting them over the head," Melian mused.

"I'm not sure that works in real life," Boral said. "Especially if they have pikes."

Melian winced. "But can't you use the pikes?"

"I can. But a trick like that is to get the door open, and I can already do that."

"What if we're thinking about this the wrong way?" Melian asked. "We can already get out. What we need is to lock them in."

"I fritz the camera, call the guards and tell them you're sick. They come in, expecting that this is a way to check on you and the camera. I mess with one of the pikes, we get past them into the hall, which normally would be stupid, except that I can override the door and fuse the lock. Then we only need a couple of minutes to get into a lifecraft." Boral nodded. "That could work."

"Let's do it," Melian said. "The longer we wait, the more chance that either Cassian and Junia will fold and jump out with us aboard or they'll fire on Beira."

"All right," Boral said. "We're on. When I mess with the pike, you just get past them and turn left down the hall. Can you act sick?"

"I promise to groan masterfully," Melian said.

"Camera first," Boral said. He closed his eyes, his hand against the wall behind him. He'd already found the node. It was just a matter of a tiny overload, a wire leading into it shorting out. Nice. "All right, we're ready." He got up and went over to the door, banging on it with his fist. "Hey! Hey! Somebody! Can you hear me? Please help! Master Melian is sick! Help!"

The door opened. One of the Marines was standing across it with a pike. "Get back," he said. Helios Melian staggered a few steps, bent over and clutching his stomach. He moaned very loudly. "Get back," the guard repeated. He held the pike horizontal, and Boral retreated before it, his hands raised, as the other Marine stepped into the room.

"What's going on?" the other Marine asked.

"He's sick!" Boral said as Melian groaned dramatically, doubling over holding onto the doorframe. Boral reached for the energy pike held by the guard in front of him. It would take too long to short it out, but activating it was easy. That was just closing a circuit.

"Yow!" the guard yelped as his pike activated.

The other Marine turned around to look at him. "What are you doing?"

And there was the current, live and fresh and inches away. *Push,* Boral thought. *That's how it's done. Just push.* The pike snapped and sizzled, the current suddenly arcing against the Marine's hand, curling suddenly purple in the air. The guard swore, dropping it as he yelled. The other Marine took a step closer. Melian was behind him. He was almost out the door.

Once more. The pike spat, a tendril zapping the other Marine's ankle. Boral charged past them, Melian ahead of him as he dashed out the door and hit the control on the other side. Normally that would hold them about a second. Boral put his hand over the panel. *Quick and dirty.* The panel blew up, wires that controlled the locking mechanism fusing.

"Let's get out of here," Boral said.

"I'm ahead of you," Melian said. They hurried down the corridor, past the first bulkhead doors. There were the yellow indicators for a lifecraft, the panel that would open if an *Abandon ship* order were given.

Boral put his hand on the panel. No alarms yet, but it wouldn't be long. There were the circuits, there the optic cables. They were meant to receive a signal that the order had been given. A quick pulse to mimic the signal…. The panel slid open, showing the airlock of the lifecraft, a little round pod big enough for four crewmembers. Melian scrambled in, gorgeous robes and all.

Boral followed. There was no need for electromancy on the interior panel. It was meant for crew abandoning ship. There were clear directions to seal the pod. "Strap in!" Boral yelled. He flung himself into the seat next to Melian. He hoped Calpurnian launch protocol wasn't much different from Morriganian. He'd done lifecraft drills. He pulled the strap across his body with one hand. The board was simple and built in. *Clear docking clamps. Disconnect umbilicals. Fire separation charge.* With a shake the lifecraft blew free, tumbling away from *Liberty*'s side. It rolled sharply, caught in Menaechmi's gravity well, stabilizing a little as it began to fall from orbit.

"We're off," Melian said. He looked vaguely ill. The lifecraft was pitching a lot.

"Yeah," Boral said. "But here comes the hard part."

"What do you mean?"

"We can't count on them to be stupid." The lifecraft was well and truly in the gravity well now, slowly rotating as it began its long fall. Boral brought the sensors online. They were in a different place than on a Morriganian craft. Why couldn't anybody do anything the same way?

"They'll notice the launch."

"They have," Boral said grimly. "Sensors are showing the aft missile tube clearing to vacuum."

"Can you get it?" Melian's voice was calm.

"Yes." He watched the board. "There's ignition. 250 live and running." He could see the streak on the little screen, the missile curving as it sought its target. "It's acquired." Boral closed his eyes. His senses were better than sensors at a certain point. There was the missile, hot and seeking, running straight toward them. He could detonate it as it came in range, but that was so close that the shrapnel would tear through the lifecraft. It wasn't a big ship with armor. Even a close hit was death.

Boral felt a cool calm sink over him, just like he'd learned, time elongating. He could see the guidance system of the mock-up missile at Sea Easting, hear his father's voice walking him through it. Guidance systems were harder than ignition or detonation, a complicated series of sensors that steered the missile, that set the target and controlled the run. It wasn't off or on. It was a whole bunch of things. Closer. The missile was getting so close. Two seconds to impact.

There. There was the cluster. Boral pushed. The missile turned, pulling out of the gravity well and streaking upward, seeking a new target. Beneath it, the lifecraft tumbled away unharmed.

"It's good to meet you too," Tal Robber said to Caralys. "Bister, what's the story?"

Bister leaned into the video frame. How to make this short and sweet? "One of the Calpurnian factions, Altissimi Cassian and Junia, have been shaking down the city of Beira. They kidnapped the Guardian's twelve-year-old kid and demanded currency and recruits. The Guardian gave them the currency and stalled on the recruits. He traded himself for his son. So right now he's a prisoner on the ship and we have the boy. Gaura Caralys wonders if the problem can be solved by renting a warship."

"I am prepared to negotiate," Caralys said. "My main goal is the protection of the city of Beira. And the other Cities of the Coast, though we're the ones being coerced."

Tal frowned. "What about your Guardian?"

Caralys's voice was even, something Bister approved of. "Of course we'd like him back, but the most important thing, to me and to him, is the protection of Beira."

Tal's eyes sought Bister's where she stood just behind Caralys. Bister nodded slightly. Yes, this was on the up and up. She meant what she said. "Well," Tal said, "We've got a slight edge on them in terms of weaponry. I'd say our presence is a deterrent...." He stopped short as something was happening in his command center behind him.

"Captain, the frigate just launched a lifecraft," someone said.

"Boral," Bister said. Caralys's hands clenched in her lap below camera level.

"Now they're launching a missile," someone said behind Tal.

"We have a 250 running, Ivory Captain."

"Battle stations!" Tal said, and through the comm Bister heard *Ivory*'s shrill alarm. "What in the name of the Lady of the Void…."

"Put Beira Control's plot on a split screen," Caralys said. They could see the icons for the ships, the missile's course. "They fired on the lifecraft," she said quietly. She didn't look away as it closed. Bister held her breath. The missile looked like it was almost on top of the lifecraft. And then it turned, making a complete U-turn and streaking back out. For a moment it ran free, then settled into a new course.

"It's acquired," Tal said. "Countermeasures! Maneuvering thrusters, hard to port. Put our nose to it."

"Slimming their profile," Bister said quietly to Caralys.

Tal must also be on the comm with the Calpurnian, because he turned. "Excuse me, are you shooting at me? Because if yes, that's a mistake." He looked over his shoulder. "Felony, clear the ventral tubes. Load and fire as they bear." On the screen *Ivory Three* was coming about, nose on to the Calpurnian, which seemed to be clawing for altitude and trying to put the curve of Menaechmi between them.

Praxi stuck his head in the door. "Gaura, Beira Control says the Morriganian scoutship is requesting immediate emergency launch clearance. What do I tell them?"

"Let them launch," Caralys said. "We have no reason to detain the Morriganians."

Praxi nodded. "I'll do that and I'm warning the merchant traffic away." As if they needed to be warned, Bister thought, with a Calpurnian frigate and *Ivory Three* slugging it out in orbit.

The screen flashed as the 250 detonated against *Ivory*'s countermeasures. Almost simultaneously *Ivory*'s missiles fired, a pair of 500s streaking toward *Liberty*. "Reload the tubes," Tal ordered. "And give me a 750 in the forward tube. Come about and stay on their tail."

"Tal, are you really planning to give them everything you've got?" Bister asked.

"They started it. They can strike and surrender if they want to," Tal said. "Come about! Come on, full thrusters!"

It was obvious even on the plot that *Ivory* wasn't turning quickly enough. *Liberty* was getting the curve of the planet between them, but the 500s were running hot. One hit countermeasures and detonated. The other went straight home, striking just forward of the ventral thruster pod. An explosion and an atmosphere plume followed.

There was a cheer on *Ivory*'s bridge. "Stick on them!" the Ivory Captain urged. "Don't let those dogs get away! Do you have a shot for the 750?"

"No, captain," a voice behind him said. "We don't have a clear run and we're losing the range."

A third symbol joined the plot, the Morriganian scoutship *Spider* rising at full boost. *Liberty* was running flat out. "Maybe they'll jump," Bister said, "as soon as they get out of the gravity well."

"Where is the lifecraft?" Caralys asked. It had dropped too low to show on the orbital plot.

Tal must have his comm screens split to pieces. "Hailing Morriganian scoutship. Whose side are you on?" There was a pause. "What do you mean you don't know?"

"Tal!" Bister said. "If you're interested in defending the City of Beira, you need to stay on this side of the planet. If you chase them, they'll come back around well before you do."

"Not on the Calpurnian side is a good answer," Tal said. "It means I don't have to shoot you. Bister, I hear you." He glanced back at someone behind them. "Disengage pursuit. Take us to four hundred kilometers and hold position above Beira."

Caralys breathed a sigh. "I'm glad you're interested in a deal, Ivory Captain." She looked at the plot, trying to find something. "Did *Liberty* jump?"

Bister shook her head. "There they are. They seem to be slowing and holding position on the other side, over your Great Southern Ocean."

"And the lifecraft?" It was completely off the plot.

The lifecraft rotated slowly, end over end, as the missile streaked away.

"You are a very handy young man to have around," Helios Melian said.

"Thanks," Boral said. He was elated. He was also not dead, which was mega-positive. "So now we land the lifecraft."

"Yes, we should do that," Melian said. Neither of them made a move toward the controls. "Aren't you going to fly this thing?"

"Me?" Boral said.

"You're starship crew."

"I'm an electromancer. A specialist, not a pilot," Boral said.

"How do you think I would know how to fly it?" Melian demanded. They looked at each other in dawning horror.

"All right," Boral said. "This thing is meant for abandoning ship, so it has to be operable by crew who aren't pilots. Starships for idiots."

"I think that covers it," Melian said. "So, two idiots in a lifecraft… That seems like the beginning of a bad joke."

"There must be an autopilot." Boral was looking around the small board. Why was everything different on Calpurnian ships?

"We need to get back to Beira."

"I know that!"

Melian reached over him. "How about this, that says *Assisted Landing*?" He touched the key and was immediately slammed back in his seat as the thruster ignited.

Boral looked at the tiny screen. "We are now heading straight for the ocean. We do not want to land in the ocean."

"Er, no," Melian said. "Can we lock onto Beira Control? They have a signal."

"I don't know how to do that!" Boral shouted. "That's a great idea except that I have no clue how we would do that! I don't even know what this stupid little map is trying to tell me because it doesn't have any labels on it!" He gestured at the tiny screen, which was showing mostly ocean and some coastline in a basic geographic scan. Everything was getting bigger fast.

Melian pointed at the graphic. "That's the coastline north of Beira. That's about where Amphi is." He glanced at Boral. "It's a coastal town that's part of Beira's territory. So Beira is just south off the bottom edge of the map. We need to turn south. How do we turn right?"

"Oh good," Boral said. "Turn right."

"Input mechanism? Voice control?" He ran his finger over the screen. "Or maybe we…" He jabbed it twice, and a star in a ring appeared on the screen at the very bottom, inland of the coast. The words *Landing Zone Set* flashed across the screen. "That was not what I meant to do," he said as the thrusters fired again. The lifecraft burned south, losing altitude fast.

"We seem to have a stalemate," Bister said. "If *Ivory Three* holds station over Beira, and *Liberty* lurks around the other side of the planet…"

"…and as it seems *Spider* is holding off in high orbit to watch…" Caralys added.

"…we're at an impasse. Tal did some damage to *Liberty*, but they're not out of the fight. If I were them, I'd cut my losses and run. But then Cassian didn't seem like a reasonable man," Bister said.

"We don't know if he has the Guardian or not," Caralys said. Her eyes didn't leave the plot screen.

"If he did, he'd be threatening to kill him," Bister said.

"There is that." Caralys shook her head. She cued the comm open to speak. "Ivory Captain, perhaps now is an opportune time to negotiate. We are willing to provide a generous payment for you to continue to provide orbital support for the City of Beira."

Bister got up and went to the door. A middle-aged disson looked over at her. "Yes?"

She dropped her voice. "There was a lifecraft launched a few minutes ago and it dropped too low for the orbital plot. Can Beira Control find it?"

They nodded. "Absolutely. I'll see where it went."

"Thank you," said Bister. She glanced back at the office where Caralys was negotiating with Tal. "Your Guardian may be aboard."

Their eyes widened. "I'll get on it."

On the good side, Boral thought, they didn't appear to be crashing in the ocean. On the bad side, they seemed to have crossed a rocky coast that didn't look like a city, huge mountains coming down almost to the sea. They were green and lush on one side, but on the other everything was brown and tan. The screen flashed. *Prepare for Landing.*

"How do we do that?" Melian demanded.

"Strap in and hang on," Boral said.

Thrusters fired suddenly to slow them. It was like hitting a brick wall, not that he'd ever hit a brick wall. The world went dark, g-forces slamming him. Inflatable baffles smacked him, filling to cushion impact. Maybe he passed out for a second. It was hard to tell. And then there was a second smack, his head swimming with dizziness. And then it was still. It was completely quiet.

There wasn't even the chirp of the board or the faint sound of the atmospheric systems. Just silence.

Boral opened his eyes. The inside of the lifecraft was dark. Not a single light showed. He could feel the baffle against his face, slowly deflating away from his body. "Guardian?" Melian had been in the seat to his right. Was he dead? Boral reached out, his hand touching a silk sleeve. There was the slight roughness of the embroidered honeybee under his fingers. "Are you all right?"

The arm moved. He heard Melian take a deep breath, then cough. "Boral?"

"Yes." Relief flooded through him. He really didn't want to be strapped in with a dead man, a man he'd probably killed by not knowing how to fly a lifecraft.

"That was unnecessary." Melian sounded as dizzy as Boral felt.

"They say any landing you can walk away from is a good one," Boral said.

"We aren't walking away yet."

"Any broken bones?" Boral flexed his arms and legs.

"If there were, don't you think I'd be screaming?" Melian asked.

"Not if you were paralyzed," Boral said.

"Are you always such a ray of sunshine?" Melian asked. "I don't seem to be paralyzed. I seem to feel every part of my body excruciatingly well."

"It's the g-forces," Boral said. "That doesn't usually cause internal bleeding."

"Thank you for that."

Boral felt he had to point something out. "You're the one who set the course!"

"You don't know how to fly either! What do they teach in the Morriganian Fleet?"

"I'm an electromancer! I've spent my whole life in a tower!" Boral shouted.

To his surprise, Melian laughed. "Well, if we're well enough to shout at each other, we're probably not dying."

"There is that," Boral said. He released his harness straps. "All right, let me see if I can get the hatch open. There doesn't seem to be much power left." He felt his way back a couple of paces to the hatch. Yeah, not a bit of power left. He couldn't feel so much as a tingle. *There must be a manual release somewhere obvious. You'd want to have that on a lifecraft. There. A handle. Pull up? Pull down?* Boral tried one and then the other. The hatch budged, a crack of bright light showing. *Right. Pump the handle.* The crack grew bigger.

Behind him, Melian had unstrapped. He hauled himself out of his seat. "Where are we?"

"I have no idea," Boral said. *Pump, pump.* The hatch opened wide enough to get through. He slid out, a cascade of sand coming in.

Melian followed him, slighter but in his elaborate robes. Boral staggered a few paces and looked back. The front end of the lifecraft was buried in sand. Ahead of them the sand stretched, dune after dune, the Greater Twin rising like a ball of fire to the east. "We're in the desert," Boral said.

Chapter Eleven

Bister had slipped out by the time Caralys finished making arrangements with the Ivory Captain. This included an immediate payment and credit on Beira's port, plus future arrangements, including the arrival of a second Name Ship from Eresh to provide added cover. It wasn't cheap to rent warships, but paying privateers was a lot less expensive than rebuilding the city, if that had even been considered an option.

Caralys took a sip of her now-cold coffee. Helios would not have approved. He had always insisted that arming would be a provocation, more of a risk than it was worth. He'd even refused Aurore's repeated pleas to arm House Melian's merchant ships. Dian agreed with Aurore, but her word didn't carry much weight with her father. Still, right now she'd have been glad if Dian had been in Beira.

Bister came in tentatively, two more cups of coffee in her hands. "I asked Beira Control to look for the lifecraft and they said they would."

Caralys took one cup gratefully. "Thank you. I hope…." She stopped. She wasn't going to consider Helios not being aboard it.

"Probably it was Boral and the Guardian," Bister said. "If they still held him, they'd be making demands." She took a sip of hers and winced. It was very hot. "They'll find them."

She had been back from her visit to the Adept for several Days when Dian came home from school. It was unclear if she had withdrawn or been asked to leave. Caralys didn't ask Helios. He was short and snappish on the entire subject. Dian moved back into her old rooms on the tenth floor and proceeded to act as if she'd never left. Which was to say, she made free with the House vehicles and property, drank as though she owned the cellars, and seemed to be continually having a party, going to a party, or sleeping it off after a party. Aurore was away tending to House business, which made it worse. Aurore at least was able to control Dian somewhat.

Getting Helios to do so seemed hopeless. It was obvious he adored "his baby girl" and that Dian could do no real wrong that involved consequences worse than yelling at her or taking away privileges for a Day. Any attempt to get him to ask where she was and what she was doing and with whom only resulted in terse comments that Dian was Dian. Caralys was on thin ice and she knew it. Helios had few immutable loyalties, but one of them was to his children. Challenging Dian was not an option.

And so she stewed, powerless. She was polite and pretty and said nothing when the arbor on the roof was full of partying twenty-year-olds all Full Night, screaming and playing unkind games that resulted in a lot of vomit on the patio and broken glass in the baths.

Helios, she thought, had a taste for parties but didn't regularly end them dead drunk. And yes, four or five old friends might join him nude in the bath, but any play that occurred was entirely consensual. She knew because she was there. It might be a sex party, but it was hardly an orgy. Those Full Nights ended with guests in comfortable sleeping closets, and if sometimes Valeri or someone else joined them on the couch, she was the only one who went to sleep next to Helios in his closet. Dawnmeal was a civilized affair in the arbor on the rooftop, watching the sun rise over Beira, eating delicious seafood and egg pies with herb sauce and toasting good fortune in orange juice with just a little nectar in it. Helios Melian was a good host. Nobody went home in tears or offense, and he certainly didn't have parties every Full Night.

Full Day was usually for sleeping or getting work done when most businesses were closed, or for the younger children. Helios was working in the study and Mia and Theo gone to bed when Caralys went down the hall to get her laundry case of clean clothes. The lift opened. Dian reeled out wearing nothing but a sequined bodysuit and a half-mask, five or six other young people with her. They all seemed wildly drunk.

"If it isn't Her Gracious Snootyness," Dian said. She glanced at the muscled young man with her. "This is Precious Vagina the High and Mighty."

"Nice to see you too, Dian," Caralys said. Her laundry case was standing behind the assistant's desk.

One of the girls seemed like she could barely stay on her feet. "I don't feel good," she said. Her pupils were dilated, and she nearly fell.

Dian reached over and pulled her strap off her shoulder, exposing one breast. The girl didn't even seem to notice. "You'll feel better once you get in the bath," Dian said.

"I don't know...."

The young man with Dian grinned. "Maybe you just need to get something in you."

"Something big," Dian said. The rest of the crew laughed.

One of the other young women pulled out her handheld. "Let's make memories, shall we?" The group reeled off toward the bath.

Caralys stood with her laundry case in her hands, hot and cold with fear. This was.... It was.... She was.... Somehow the phrase never completed itself. *You have more power than half of Beira,* Adrian had said, and yet she didn't have the power to walk down the hall past the door of the bath.

Or did she? Suddenly she could see just how to do it. An absolute chill descended around her. She could see how to stop this, not just tonight but for a long time to come. She walked down the hall, her feet leaving deep imprints in the thick carpet, through the sitting room, and into the study.

Helios looked up from the screen, a headset on to dictate a communication while he scrolled through information. He was wearing a long white tunic, the embellished neckline the only ornament. "Are you still working?" Caralys said charmingly. She put her laundry case down. "Darling, don't you think that's enough for today?"

"I'm trying to finish…" he began.

She leaned over his shoulder and gave him a kiss, as deep and intoxicating as she knew how, with just a tiny nibble of tongue. "And leaving me all alone," she said as she straightened up. "I suppose I'll have to take a bath all by myself."

He looked gobsmacked as usual. "Well, I suppose I could put it away until Greater Day."

"I suppose you could," Caralys said sweetly. "I'm just going to put this in my closet. Why don't you run on to the bath and I'll be there in a minute? We could wash each other's backs and get all the dirt off."

Helios smirked. "That seems like a very good idea. I'll see you in a moment." He started off down the hall toward the bath.

Carefully, Caralys picked up her laundry case and carried it into her sleeping closet. Two minutes. Maybe three. Four at the outside. She took a deep breath, then went back through the study and the sitting room. She could hear the clamor from there. Helios was shouting. Dian was shouting back. As she opened the door to the hall the young man was streaking for the lift, one of the young women following. The doors closed on them.

Caralys went to the door of the bath. The girl she'd seen earlier was sagging on Helios, makeup running down her face, nude from the waist up. She was sobbing while Helios held her up and he was screaming. "…I never expected this from you! You disgrace House Melian and you disgrace me! You dishonor the goddess whose gifts have been so lavishly given to us!"

Dian was standing stunned. "But Daddy, she said she'd party with us…."

"You know perfectly well that whatever you've given her, she's not lucid," Helios yelled.

"It's just a party drug," Dian said. "We…"

He saw Caralys. "Cara, will you find the rest of this young lady's clothes and see her home? Make sure she's all right?"

"Yes, of course," Caralys said. She found the blush-colored top by the pool, soaking wet. Well, there was a spare shirt of hers on the dressing hooks. She gently disengaged the girl from Helios. "Come on, darling," she said softly. "Come on."

The girl gulped. "I never said—"

"Yes, sweetheart," Caralys said, leading her out of the bath and out of Dian's sight. "I know. I've been you." She helped her into the dry cover-up, a long dark blue shirt that reached below her knees. Caralys was much taller. "It's all right. We're leaving now. Do you have your shoes?"

"Yes?" She looked down. Her eyes seemed to be focusing better now.

"Diamond or Glitterpowder?" Caralys asked as she got her into the lift. The street names came back easily.

"Glit, I think," the girl said. "We were at this club and they asked if I wanted to party with them and I thought…."

"I know how it works," Caralys said. "But that crew is bad news. Whether they promised you a good time or actually currency, it's a bad deal." The lift doors opened at the garage level. "Can you walk?"

"I think so." She wiped her face on her sleeve, makeup smearing the cover-up.

Caralys waved her rings over the lock to the garage doors. She could take the small private vehicle. It was parked on the outside and she wouldn't have to wake a driver. She winged open the doors remotely and helped the girl into the passenger side. "Here we go. Just breathe through it. We'll go home now."

It was nearly two hours before she got back, the hot double suns of Full Day beating down on the streets of Beira when she pulled back into the garage. The corridor was quiet. Helios was in his study. He wasn't working. He was looking out the window grimly, having changed out of his damp shirt into a dark blue one and matching loose pants. He glanced around when Caralys came in but said nothing.

"I took the girl home," Caralys said quietly. "She was pretty much through it when I left; Glit, she thought. And the rest of it—it could have been a lot worse. Would have been, if you hadn't come in." Caralys paused. "It wasn't a wealthy home."

Helios shook his head once. The lines around his mouth were deep-graven. "She was such a radiant child," he said. It took Caralys a moment to realize he meant Dian, not the girl. "She was a ray of light, bold and bright and irrepressible." He leaned against the glass, looking out toward the sea. "Phoebe and I divorced when she was six. It was amicable. We wanted different things at forty than we had at twenty-eight. Phoebe has House membership. She moved to an apartment downstairs. A few years later she married Leo. Aurore and Dian ran back and forth. Dian seemed to get along with Lyra well enough when I married her. I don't know what happened."

Caralys came to stand at the window with him but didn't touch. It wasn't the time.

"I've tried to be understanding. I've said that it was youthful foibles. I've said that she was just a little immature. But this. This is despicable in the eyes of the gods." He shook his head like an old animal in a trap. "Consent is the basis of license. It's the bedrock of contracts. That's what they're for. Everyone agrees on what the boundaries are. Everyone knows what is and isn't off-limits. They're there for everyone's protection, but especially for the poorer signatory. That's why at the start of every Day there is a line in the magistrate's office of tourists paying fines because they didn't read the contract in full. It's there to protect the sex worker."

"She's not in the Guild or anything else," Caralys said quietly. "She's just a kid who does pickups with people with currency."

Helios shook his head again. "And what kind of Guardian am I, with this under my own roof?"

"One who loves his daughter," Caralys said. It had hurt him. She had hurt him. But he would have never believed her if she had just told him. He had to see. He had to feel.

"I don't know what to do," Helios said. He looked down at his immaculately groomed hands. "The point of a contract is consent."

"Mine says I consent to anything requested short of physical harm," Caralys said. She hadn't quite meant to say it. She stopped before she added, *You know the rules don't apply to the rich.*

He looked at her sideways. "You know I would not have written a contract like that."

"It's the contract you took over," Caralys said gently. "And yes, you have never required anything of me I did not consent to. But you could."

"I wouldn't."

"I know that too." She put her hand on his arm. "But what Dian sees is that you could. She doesn't know what actually passes between us. She only knows what the paper says. It says I am yours to do with as you wish."

"I have never held you to any part of the contract against your wishes." Helios frowned. "Or at least I think I haven't. Certainly not to any wishes you expressed. And silliness like claiming that your clothing and shoes are my property rather than yours…. Your personal property belongs to you."

"And you give me a salary despite the contract stipulating that I do not need to be paid but may be tipped if you wish it," Caralys said. "You simply call it a tip. And the pregnancy clause…." She stopped.

His frown deepened. "I hope you know that I would never require you to end a pregnancy because of the contract. I would never do that. If you chose to have a child, I would welcome it. You do know that, don't you?"

She had been almost certain. She put her head on his shoulder. "I do," she said. "My dear, you have never treated me badly. But how would Dian know that? And what is the difference between a gaura's contract and a marriage contract except duration and the amount of the financial settlement? Both can be broken for misconduct." She watched his face change and realized she'd stepped in it, stepped in something.

"Or for deception and false pretense," Helios said. "Misconduct is preferable, don't you think?"

Caralys took a breath. "What did you deceive her about?"

"You're a clever woman. Haven't you figured it out by now?" His voice was falsely light.

She knew. It was written all over him. "Which relative?" she asked quietly.

"My grandmother." He glanced away, over the sun-bathed roofs of the city, glaring in Full Day. "Lyra…Lyra didn't know. I didn't think it would matter. And then there was the signing of the marriage contract. A disclaimer. Boilerplate for a Great House marriage, they said. All the Great Houses require it."

"Yes," Caralys said softly. "They do." She'd always known that. And of course he did think it would matter. You don't lie about something that doesn't matter.

"An affidavit that I have no Merrow blood to the fifth generation. What was I to say in a room full of attorneys and Lyra and her family? I signed it." He didn't take his eyes off the cityscape, tall buildings nearby giving way to the huddle of shorter ones in the storm surge zone.

"You lied," she said.

"Under oath. And of course she found out." Helios shook his head. "When my father died. I wasn't head of House Melian when we were married. My father was in his nineties. I'd been running the business for years while he was comfortably retired. We always got on well. I'd ask his advice and he'd give it and never know if I took it or not. But when he died the house was full of elderly relatives and some of them talked too freely." He glanced at her, then away again. "They didn't know Lyra didn't know. Phoebe was there. She knew. Aurore knew. Everybody knew but Lyra." He took a deep breath, his throat working. "This was when she was pregnant with Mia. Lyra was…distraught. She wanted to induce immediately even though she was only halfway through the pregnancy to get this tainted flesh out of her body. She wouldn't so much as look at the baby. And it was…" He stopped, closing his eyes.

Caralys stepped closer, putting her arm around his waist, leaning her head against his shoulder. "My dear, you can't imagine it would matter to me."

He didn't open his eyes. "Why wouldn't it?"

"Not everyone with old blood is a bigot."

He put his arm around her and held her tight, tight as she was holding him. With his face against her hair she couldn't see his expression at all. "I was desperate to keep Theo from knowing. From understanding why his mother didn't want him anymore. He was three. I had to keep Theo safe."

"So you staged a reason for divorce and gave her everything she wanted in exchange for her silence," Caralys said. It all made sense now, why Phoebe had House membership and Lyra didn't, why she never saw the children. "A divorce contract that stipulated that her generous settlement depended on never speaking of it."

"Yes." He took a deep breath. "I understand she lives in Casera now. She's married again. I have no reason to contact her. After all, it was a business arrangement that went badly." His voice caught a little. "She said that of course she'd never loved me. It was simply business—my money for her family connections, respectability for an upstart House. She discovered the contract wasn't what it appeared. What else would one expect in the Great Houses? Marriages are business deals."

And you loved her, Caralys thought. *You loved her with all your warm, generous heart and you thought that you could win her. You thought you could charm her and sweeten her and even if she married you for currency, sooner or later she'd fall in love with you. And of course you were wrong, my darling. That's not how the Great Houses are, not the old aristocracy.*

"Dian was fourteen," Helios said. "She adored Lyra. Lyra had gotten her into a very expensive academy that Lyra had gone to. She worshipped Lyra. Everything Lyra did was wonderful and everything Phoebe did was pedestrian and lower-class. Having Lyra suddenly cut off was very painful." He sighed. "I suppose I let Dian get away with too much. I didn't want to come down on her for hurting when it was my fault she was hurt."

Caralys tightened her arms around him. "And you hurt."

"Nonsense. It was a business deal gone bad." She couldn't see his face.

"So you spent three years partying and then bought out the contract of a gaura so that you literally held all the power," Caralys said. *So that no one could ever hurt you again.*

"A contract binds two ways, my love," he said. "I'd spent three years never seeing the same person for more than a Day. A contract meant I had to give you a chance."

"Oh," she said. And she'd taken it, hadn't she? She'd worked her way into every corner of his life, including maybe his heart. There was something she had to make clear. She pulled back, enough that she could meet his eyes. "Helios, I would never, ever do that. I would never hold your blood against you and I would never hurt your children. I wouldn't do that even if we were never speaking again. That is not who I am."

"I know, Cara." The corner of his mouth twisted. "You're a kind person. Kindness, sweetness and joy are underrated."

And she'd manipulated him into catching Dian in the act. But otherwise it would have just gone on, one person or another, and now at least that might stop. "I am not as kind as you think," Caralys said, but she held him tight, knowing her power. It was heavy.

Two Days later, she was closing up her work at the start of Full Night when she noticed that one of the House trundles had logged into the garage but no one had come up. Frowning, Caralys called it, but no one answered. "Show the garage camera," she told her handheld.

The trundle was there. Beside it, kneeling on the concrete was a young woman vomiting, her head down and her back heaving. "Oh, not again," Caralys said. She put her shoes on and hurried down to rescue Dian's latest victim. The lift opened. She went out into the garage. The young woman looked up, smeared glitter and ruined clothes. It was Dian.

For a moment Caralys froze. Dian closed her eyes. "Go away," she said quietly. "Just go away. I can't deal with anything more right now."

Caralys didn't move from the step. Fear held her paralyzed. "What's happened?"

"It's none of your business," Dian said, her eyes closed. "Like you care what happens to me. You'd be happy to see me gone. You're turning my father against me and there isn't anything I can do to stop you. So you win. Good Caralys wins. Bad Dian loses." She sat back against the trundle, her eyes closed.

I promise I would never hurt your children. Her own words trapped her. She didn't move from the step. "Where have you been?" she asked, her voice sounding even and timbreless.

"House Granico," Dian said without opening her eyes. "Talitha Granico's party. If you've heard of her."

Flashing lights, bright strobes, holding very still while Talitha brandished a dildo, everybody laughing. It won't require medical treatment. It doesn't violate the contract. House Granico held her indenture….

Caralys put her hand on the smooth concrete wall. "I've heard of her," she said. Something shifted. She'd been twenty-three, not eighteen. And suddenly there was no monster in the garage, just a sad little bundle of torn chiffon and smeared makeup, a girl seven years her junior who sat huddled beside the trundle in the middle of the night. "I know her," Caralys said. "Why were you there? You didn't have to be."

Her eyes opened, blazing, the anger again. "I have to be somewhere! Where do you think I can go? I can't keep taking up less and less space. I have to have some friends. I have to have some kind of life. Somebody has to care."

"Your father cares for you very much," Caralys said.

Dian laughed. "You don't know. He doesn't. He just wants me out of the way, like Lyra did. She said she loved me and I was so special and so pretty and wonderful, and it was all just to smarm up to my dad. She didn't mean any of it. I wrote to her and wrote to her and wrote to her after the divorce and she never answered. I begged." She broke off in a sob. "Just because Daddy cheated on her all over the place. And he lied to her. I won't even tell you what it was about."

"I know," Caralys said. "He told me."

Dian snorted. "Great. He told you. He didn't tell me. He let me find out from school when they threw me out."

"That was a mistake." She came closer, sitting down on the end of the step. "I think he meant to tell you when you were older."

And now it wasn't cold. She wasn't afraid. This was no different than the friends she'd comforted in the middle of the night.

"Yeah, well, he didn't." Dian leaned her head back against the trundle. "And it's supposed to be a secret, so I have to worry about every single person I know and when they'll find out and what will happen. And you know what will happen. The minute it comes out everybody will loathe me."

"Everybody in that crowd, maybe," Caralys said. That was unfortunately true.

"Well, this is the crowd I have to live with," Dian said. "The Best People. The kids of the Great Houses. The people I'm going to be seeing across the dinner table and boardroom table for the rest of my life. I'm going to have to marry one of them. I'm going to have to spend my entire life waiting for it to come out. I wish I could just rip it out of me. I wish I didn't know. At least then I could be happy until they find out."

Caralys let out a long breath. "I wish I could say you're wrong," she said. "But you're not. They're terrible and they will be cruel."

Dian looked at her as if surprised Caralys had agreed. "So what am I supposed to do? Aurore wants to just tell everybody preemptively and let them hate her. Daddy says that we can't tell anybody and that if Aurore does it will hurt Theo and Mia and probably mean he can't be Guardian anymore. Where am I supposed to go? I can't fit in a smaller box."

"I don't know," Caralys said carefully. "But I do know this. Most people in Beira aren't like the Best People."

"People with power are."

"There are different kinds of power," Caralys said. "Money and an old name are two kinds. But there are other kinds too. Personally, I'd like to grind the Best People into dust." There was an edge in her voice that wasn't hapalia, an echo of the screams she'd aimed at Adrian.

"There isn't anybody else."

"There isn't anybody else you know," Caralys said. She sighed. "And that's at your father's door, isn't it? He let Lyra send you to a private school. He hasn't had you move in less rarified circles."

"I wanted to go to the school," Dian said. "I liked it there. Until Lyra told them and they kicked me out in the middle of the day when I was thirteen. She told them and they told me that I was leaving and someone would pack my room and send it after. I couldn't even pack it myself. Merrow aren't allowed in the dormitory."

"That's horrible," Caralys said. "But not surprising."

"And I came home and Lyra had already left without saying goodbye and Mia was in the natal center because she was induced really premature and I lost all my friends and Daddy didn't care." Her face crumpled. "He didn't care." Caralys put her arm around her, and after a moment Dian gulped. "I'm nothing but a bother to him and he has you and he spends all his time with you and all I want is my Mom back. I want Lyra back! She pretended to love me. I want someone to pretend to love me. Is that too much to ask?"

"No, darling. Not at all." Caralys ducked her head against Dian's. So like her father. So much like Helios, who hired someone to pretend to love him.

"And this…." She gestured at the clothes, at the puddle by the trundle. "It's like being loved for a little while. When somebody's sexing me at least I'm not being ignored."

Caralys hunted for the words. "He didn't mean to. He'd just lost his father, and then there was Mia premature, and the divorce on top of that. He was just overwhelmed. It's not that he didn't love you. There just wasn't enough of him to go around. And you and Aurore were older. It seemed like you needed him less than Mia and Theo did." She squeezed Dian's shoulder. "And that wasn't true."

Dian shivered. It all seemed to keep pouring out. "When he bought your contract, I thought that if we had a gaura at least there would be somebody I could sex with who was paid to be nice to me. I mean, that's all there is, right? You pay people to fix your hair or be your counselor and listen to you and pretend they care about you when you're just a job to them. But at least a gaura would be around and you might be nice to me. But no. You're all for him. Just like everything is all for him."

"I'm not being paid to be nice to you now, am I?" Caralys asked.

"No." Dian straightened up, looking at her curiously. "Why are you?"

"Maybe because I've been lost too." She took a deep breath. "My parents died when I was young. I've never had anyone to turn to who had any power to help me. I have friends, but my friends are dancers and young artists and costumers who live out of their pocket with nothing in the bank. Until Helios." She stopped. "I'm not Lyra. And I'm not going to be Lyra. I'm not going to choose to hurt any of you and I'm not going to use my power to cause more damage."

"What?"

She could see how to drive the wedge. She could see how to make Dian leave forever. And she could see how not to. "I have been very lucky," Caralys said, "so I should be kind." She squeezed Dian's shoulder. "Now, we're going to go in and find your father."

It was several hours before Helios came to bed. He had sat up with Dian in the salia talking until the first hint of dawn came in the sky. Caralys sat up in the study, curled up on the couch attempting to watch a comedy on the screen. He looked tired, coming in and shutting the door. "Dian's finally gone to bed," he said. He sat down on the end of the couch. "She doesn't want me to do anything about the people tonight. She says it will make that social set reject her if she says they assaulted her. I have no idea what to do with that." He put his head in his hands..

"She needs a different social set," Caralys said bluntly. "The rich are cruel."

"I should never have sent her to that school."

"It's not just the school." Caralys heard the anger in her own voice. "You don't behave this way so you don't imagine that others do. It's how the powerful behave. She is rich. She is the daughter of the Guardian. She has no choice about that!"

He looked up. "And should I give up my power? Is that the price? Is that what will satisfy her? If I resign and give her everything?"

"No, you should not resign!" Caralys said exasperatedly. "You should take away their privileges! And I know you can't. You can't outlaw private schools, those nasty incubators of cruelty. You can't make them less awful."

"Isn't that what I do? When I tax their fortunes and favor the Guild members instead of the old Houses and quietly transfer power and money away from them?" Helios snapped. "But I can't do that without power myself."

"And that is why I respect you as well as love you."

He stopped, shaking his head. He reached for her foot under the throw, stroking it to touch her. "Cara, I don't know what to do. I should never have married Lyra, but that's done. There's nothing I can do to fix it. I can't make Dian to have gone to a different school where she met normal people. I can't make our Merrow blood disappear or make everyone accept it. I can't make up the attention she needed when she was thirteen. I can't even smack those little shits in the mouth without making it worse for her."

"No, you can't do any of those things." She scooted down the couch so that he could lean on her. "But you can love her and spend time with her now and introduce her to people who aren't part of that poisonous social set."

"True." Helios took a deep breath. "I can introduce her to some actual adults who behave like adults."

"And she needs a mistress," Caralys said. Helios blinked. "Someone older than she is who has some experience with the world outside that bubble and who is basically a kind and stable person. Someone who will give her uncomplicated sex and someone to go places with that aren't wild parties. And the last thing she needs is someone her own age who is a mess of issues or completely innocent. She's too much like you, my dear."

"I see that." He bent his head. "I can certainly afford one for her. If you think that will help."

"I think she will have no interest in partying with this crowd if she can do something more fun with someone she likes more," Caralys said. "Someone trustworthy, maybe an artist or entertainer who would love to have a young, exciting patron. They would introduce her to a different world and there would be a contract for the security of all parties." She kissed the top of his head. "And your attention, my dear. You can't go back in time, but you can give it now. I can share."

"You are the most generous person I've ever known," he said, and buried his face against her shoulder. This time the power that rested on her wasn't heavy.

Chapter Twelve

Boral looked around the desert with a kind of despair. He knew about deserts on Morrigan. Basically, if you went there, you died unless you had all kinds of special equipment. Which they didn't. Helios Melian, however, seemed less disturbed. He climbed up the nearest dune and looked around, shading his eyes with his hand, his gorgeous blue and gold robes utterly incongruous.

Boral climbed up to stand next to him. To the east, dunes continued as far as the eye could see, perhaps broken with some low brown hills of barren stone thrust up through the dunes like islands in a sea of sand. To the west, a long chain of mountains rose, their sides covered in brown scrub, the peaks to the north snowcapped. The nearest mountain was huge, its peak shrouded in cloud. "Do you have any idea where we are?" Boral asked.

"Yes, actually." Melian looked relieved. "That's the Old Man. We're on the wrong side of the mountains, but not more than about forty kilometers from Beiran territory." He looked toward the east. "The Lesser Twin is rising, and this currently comfortable temperature is going to increase, but it won't be Full Day until the Greater Twin rises, and that won't be for nine hours or so."

Boral took a deep breath. "There are probably some emergency supplies in the lifecraft. Ours have them. I guess the Calpurnians do too. Somebody probably saw the lifecraft land. If we just stay with it, they'll pick us up eventually."

"I'm sure someone did," Melian said. He was looking off to the southeast. "Which is why we can't stay with it. These are Merrow lands."

"What?" Boral asked.

Melian took off his long, embroidered vest. "Let's get the emergency supplies and start walking." He headed back toward the lifecraft, Boral following after.

"Walk where?" Boral said. "Why?"

Melian stopped. "To Beiran Territory. Which is that way. The Old Man is in Beiran Territory. This side of the mountain is a nature reserve, but there are waystations and patrols and seismic observation stations. And as to why, because we are in the territory of a hostile power and our presence here is provocation for war. It behooves us to leave as quickly as possible."

"I don't understand," Boral said. "I thought the other Cities of the Coast were south of here."

"They are." Melian gestured impatiently. "But the interior of the continent belongs to the Merrow. Our demarcation line is along the edge of the mountains. I have promised that under no conditions will any Beiran enter their territory, and that should that happen the Merrow have the full right to impose any punishment they see fit, short of execution. It's a very long story. The import of it is that we are in violation of that treaty. I am in violation of my own treaty, which is at the least a serious incident and at worst a trigger for hostilities. So we need to leave. Now."

"Fine." Boral hunted around inside the lifecraft for emergency supplies. Yes, there were knapsacks with the usual emergency symbols on them. A quick glance inside showed water pouches, wound kits, nutrition packets, and more. "Let's go then. Sure. We can walk forty kilometers across the desert."

"I didn't say I'd like to," Melian said. He looked old and tired to Boral. "But the Merrow most certainly saw the lifecraft land. We'd have been visible for hundreds of kilometers. They'll come to investigate." He put his carefully folded vest on top in one of the knapsacks. "Fortunately, so will Beirans. We walk toward the Old Man and hope that the Beirans find us before the Merrow do."

"Right, then," Boral said. At least it wasn't hard to figure out where they were going. There was the mountain, right there. They couldn't miss it. And if Melian was up for a desert trek at his age, Boral could be. Not that hiking was something you did either at a tower or in the Fleet. He could pull enough electricity out of the ambient, maybe, to use the lifecraft's systems to send a signal, but he bet that Melian would say that it was too dangerous and these Merrow would know exactly where they were. So it was time to start hiking.

He put his knapsack on his shoulder and started walking. "So why does Cassian want you to give him recruits? It doesn't make any sense. Calpurnia isn't short on population."

Melian looked at him sideways, a little smile on his face. "Now that's a very interesting question. He has one ship…"

"…a frigate," Boral put in, "which isn't much for someone claiming to be a grand admiral."

"Exactly. How many crew would you say a frigate carries? Normally."

Boral shrugged. "A hundred and fifty, maybe two hundred. You could operate with less, but you'd generally want fifty or so on a watch, and then some specialists like me who aren't duplicated around the clock. If you had to, you could probably operate with fifty or sixty, but they'd be overworked."

"Useful information," Melian said. He looked off across the desert. "And under what circumstances would fifty untrained recruits be helpful?"

"If you were so short-handed you couldn't give people at least watch on, watch off," Boral said. "I mean, otherwise they'd be more trouble than they were worth. There aren't a lot of jobs on a starship that aren't skilled. You could put them in shipboard services, I guess. That might free up some people who knew more. I sure wouldn't want to ship with them."

"And why would a starship be so short-handed?"

Melian looked like he genuinely appreciated Boral's expertise, which felt good, so he went on. "I'm guessing," he said, "but the amount of battle damage I saw when we came aboard wouldn't account for it. I mean, you don't lose half your crew that way. It's not enough damage to cause that number of casualties. It's just not. Which means they left somehow."

"Jumped ship," Melian mused. "Or perhaps Cassian and his followers took the ship with their loyalists instead of the regular crew."

"That makes sense," Boral said slowly. "If the ship was docked for repair or refit, you could take the ship with just a few people. There wouldn't be more than ten or so aboard as a chain watch. If you had fifty or sixty, you could definitely fly it out of there, but it really wouldn't be functional as a warship." He looked at Melian. "Is that what you think happened?"

"It might have." He looked thoughtful. "It would make sense, given the political situation on Calpurnia."

"So Cassian killed Iulus? Or something like that?" It had all been very complicated. In the aftermath of the battle he hadn't been paying attention to what had happened on Calpurnia.

"Iulus was assassinated after he returned from Morrigan," Helios Melian said. "Cassian and the Politist faction claimed responsibility." Melian looked at him like that was supposed to mean something.

"Er," Boral said.

"There are three main groups in Calpurnian politics today. You can call them factions, but they're more like ideologies—beliefs about how people should live."

"I know what an ideology is," Boral said. "My father had us read about it. Um, the other two are Social Logic and…"

"The Federationists," Melian said. "About ninety years ago, the Federationists and the Politists fought it out in the Internal War. For most of the time since then, the Politists have been on top. The Social Logic faction is the new one, the reformers. Altissima Gnea was their champion."

"Only she got killed trying to take Eresh," Boral said.

"Exactly." Melian paused at the top of a sand dune. "So then Iulus was the most powerful and he was a Federationist. But he was assassinated by the Politists."

"So who's in charge now?" Boral asked.

Melian stopped for a moment, glancing upwards. "The situation is murky. But Cassian's presence here, probably on the run, strongly suggests it's not the Politists. I've played one faction against another for years, which has kept them out of Beira except for demands for money. But my last deal was with the Federationists, and Cassian clearly sees no reason to honor it."

"Does the Warlady know all this?" Boral asked.

"I would be stunned if she didn't," Melian said with a quick smile. "I assume her intelligence is as good as mine."

Boral considered. "I think so," he said. There must be Morriganian spies on Calpurnia. Surely. "Probably most of the Calpurnian Navy went back to Calpurnia," he said slowly. "I mean, they kind of had to jump out randomly, wherever they could get a plot." The last part of the battle had been chaotic, after they got a missile through the side of *Spider*'s mess. To Boral it had seemed like a lot of missile defense, things being thrown at him constantly until he was so tired, knowing he had to focus and get just one more, and then eventually it stopped. He'd laid down on his jump couch and closed his eyes. Paloma had woken him up when they finished docking at Orbital Three. He'd gone to sleep just like that for more than two hours, right in the command center with everything going on.

"Certainly Iulus did," Melian said. "And my sources suggest that quite a few ships did as well. However, my factor on Lono said that there were a number of vessels there as well under the command of one of Iulus's lieutenants, Antisia."

"You have intelligence from Lono?" Helios Melian seemed remarkably well informed for someone who theoretically was only the Guardian of a single city.

"That's where my ship, *Light Dancer*, was returning from when it was stopped by Cassian. And it's not secret if anyone can see it. Any ship landing at Tranquility can see that there are Calpurnian naval vessels in port. Surely your Warlady knows this."

"Yeah," Boral said. She probably did, but he bet she'd find it interesting anyway. He thought this through. "So the Federationists have Lono, and the Politists are on the run. So who's in charge on Calpurnia? Social Logic?"

Melian looked like Boral's father did when he figured out some thorny problem. "That's the question, isn't it?"

Caralys was arranging a currency transfer to pay the Ivory Captain when Bister came back in again. She'd been popping in and out of the office. Caralys frowned at the screen. House Melian's discretionary account had been emptied to pay the Altissimi. This needed to come out of Beira's accounts since the privateers were hired to protect the city, not House Melian. Which meant a number of extremely diplomatic conversations with Beira's treasury staff. Fortunately, the Vice-Adjutant was a close adherent of Helios despite being from one of the richest Great Houses. She rather liked him. "Paying a privateer is cheaper than any other alternative, and you know it," Caralys said. "It will provide a deterrent to another Calpurnian attempt at extortion at the very least."

Bister seemed to be trying to get her attention. "Can you hold a moment, Arsenio? I have an urgent interruption." She turned the mic off. "Yes, Bister?"

"Beira Control has a landing plot on the lifecraft," Bister said. "It activated steering thrusters and made a safe landing here." She pointed to the plot on the handheld screen she had. "Send a flyer to pick them up?"

Caralys looked at the device and took a deep breath. Her heart sank. "No," she said. "That's not possible." Of course there was yet another problem. "We need to send an all-terrain trundle instead. There are some at the patrol stations near the summit of the Old Man."

"A flyer would be faster," Bister said. She looked perplexed.

"They're well inside Merrow territory," Caralys said. "A trundle won't be noticed as easily. Tell Praxi to get on that right now. The sooner the better; one vehicle, with experienced rangers who know how to keep their heads down. We don't need more than one war at a time."

Boral slogged along through the sand. It wasn't that hot yet. Hot enough that he was sweating, but not so hot he was going to pass out like people on Morrigan did on the Light Side. You'd pass out in minutes, they said, and then just roast until you died. But it wasn't that hot here, and Melian didn't seem to think it would be. He looked tired and hot and he'd taken off the long silk tunic and bundled it into Boral's bag, wearing just a lightweight blue gauze shirt under it.

"Why did you paint your fingernails gold?" Boral asked.

"Because it matches my outfit," Melian said.

Boral shook his head. "No, I mean why do you make your fingernails a different color than the rest of you?"

Melian stopped. "What?"

Boral held out his hands, chewed nails and all. "I mean, why nails?"

Melian shrugged. "We just do. It's being hapalos. I don't usually wear much color anymore—too young and trendy. I generally wear gold or simply a clearcoat manicure."

Boral felt like he understood about three words of that. "We don't do that on Morrigan."

"So I see." Melian sounded amused. They walked on for a few minutes. "You are doing as your father said and having experiences."

"I'm not sure this was what he had in mind," Boral said. On the other hand, it certainly was an experience. "I think I'm learning a lot about other cultures," he said seriously. It wasn't clear to him why Melian started laughing.

"I am sure that you are," Melian said. "And I am certain he will be very proud of you."

"I hope so," Boral said. What exactly he'd say was murky. He hoped it didn't involve the words 'You can't go anywhere ever again.' But it probably wouldn't if they just got back to Beira and he returned to the ship without anymore trouble.

Melian had stopped. "Oh, that's not good," he said. A vehicle was coming toward them, desert colored on caterpillar treads, no larger than a trundle but buttoned up tight against sun and sand alike. "Get your hands up," Melian said. "And do not, under any circumstances, say my name or who I am."

"Why not?" Boral asked, raising his arms.

"Because they think Helios Melian is the Infernal Lord himself." He raised his arms as well, bareheaded under the bright sky.

The vehicle came closer. And closer. Just when Boral thought it was going to hit them, it stopped. Doors opened and four people got out. It was impossible to guess whether they were men or women. They wore loose trousers, long jackets and boots in all the colors of the desert, and helmets with mirrored masks built in to cut the glare. Not an inch of their skin showed, nor anything to give any clue to their identities.

And they were carrying projectile rifles. Boral sucked in a breath. Projectile rifles were old tech, never used on starships, and on Morrigan nobody in the general population carried any kind of weapon except a blade. Knives and swords were legal; nothing else was. But the big thing about projectile rifles was that there was nothing electronic about them. Boral had nothing to work with. "Oh no," he said under his breath.

If Melian heard him, he gave no indication of it. He smiled broadly, his hands raised. "We are glad to see you, travelers! I give you respectful greetings in the name of the Third Lord!"

The one in front took a step toward him, close enough to seem menacing, the mirrored shade over their face reflecting the harsh light. "Do not sully His name with your tongue!"

Melian didn't move. "I would not speak the name which must not be spoken, but only greet you in the remembrance of His peace. We are here by sad accident and seek nothing more than to leave and return to our own place under His Covenant of Mercy."

Boral stood very still. A second figure joined the first. "You know something of the Covenant, traveler. Why?"

"My grandmother was of your people," Melian said. "And though she died long ago, I keep the words she spoke to me with reverence." He inclined his head. "The boy and I were captured from a Beiran starship by the Calpurnians and made our escape. We did not intend to land in your territory. Surely your Wise have monitored the nets and have seen this for yourselves if you tracked our lifecraft."

The first one spoke again. "Are you both men?"

"Yes," Melian said. "We are."

"It is hard to tell with you. Show us."

"Of course." Melian looked at Boral as he unfastened his trousers. "Boral, show them you're male."

Boral unfastened his pants, his face hot. The second figure took a quick look at the equipment. Then they nodded, stepping back and taking off their helmet. Or his helmet. The face beneath was a young man no older than Boral, with a light brown beard and green eyes. He smiled. "If we're all men, it's all good. You give us no uncleanness."

"Um, yeah," said Boral, closing his pants back up.

"You're lucky it was us, not a group from a Women's Community," he said. "They'd have to shoot you."

"Sure," Boral said.

Melian was speaking the first one. "...and so we found a lifecraft and launched under fear of death. We were not able to choose our place of landing more correctly."

The first one put his hands on his hips. "You seem awfully soft for a starship crewman."

"It is true," Melian said, "that I am not a starship crewman. I am a factor, an accountant. I keep books, and I was returning from an audit on Lono. The boy is apprenticed as an engineer. We were held together as we were both considered to pose little danger."

The first took off his helmet; he was sandy-haired and perhaps thirty. He scrubbed his hands through his hair. "You wear blue and the boy wears the honeybee device. You work for Helios Melian?"

"I work for House Melian."

The sandy haired man clenched his jaw. "And how do you justify his robbery of our precious Community? Of the children he corrupts?"

Melian spread his hands. "Traveler, I know nothing of these matters. I am an accountant who has worked most recently on Lono."

The young man with Boral shrugged and spat on the sand away from him. "You work for the pervert too?"

"I guess," Boral said. He thought he'd better start embroidering. "My father trained me as best he could, and he sent me on the starship telling me to do my best and obey my superiors and make him proud. I'm trying to do that. And not get killed."

"Yeah, good plan," the guy said. "You like working on a starship?"

"Oh yeah," Boral said. "It's pretty good. You go all kinds of interesting places."

"Like where?"

"Morrigan," Boral said. "I've been to Morrigan."

The young guy dropped his voice. "Are there any girls on the starship?"

Boral nodded. He spoke quietly too. "Oh yeah. Lots of girls. Like about half the crew."

"What's it like? Working with girls? What do they look like?"

"Um?" Red and Paloma sprang immediately to mind. "Just like girls, I guess."

Melian was going on. "All we ask is that we be allowed to continue on our way. We will leave your territory as quickly as possible and never return. We know our presence on your lands is offensive and we are contrite."

"Why should we let you do that when you offend us?" the sandy-haired man asked.

"Is it not revealed that if your brother ask your pardon, you must give it?" Melian asked. "I humbly ask your pardon for my presence and will remedy my offense if you will allow it."

"You're awfully glib," he replied. "Are there those who still wait for the Sand Wave?"

Melian nodded. "Who know that the earth will rise up and swallow the seas in the end of days? Yes, there are those who believe that."

"And you?" The sandy-haired man raised his chin.

"I am an accountant," Melian said. "I am not disrespectful enough to imagine that I know the Third Lord's mind." He met the man's eyes, guileless and honest. "I am nobody in His sight."

The sandy-haired man nodded slowly. "All right. You and the boy can go. Start walking. And if we ever see you again," he patted his rifle, "you'll learn what it means to be on our lands."

Melian nodded. "Thank you. May the Covenant of Mercy guide your steps."

"And guide yours straight out of our lands."

"Come on, Boral," Melian said. "Now."

"Good luck," the young guy said. "Take care now."

"You too," Boral said, and hurried after Melian as fast as he could.

He waited until they were a good distance away, the men back in their vehicle and its engine running. They turned it in the opposite direction, heading toward the lifecraft. "What just happened?" he demanded. "Who are they? What was that about? Why did they want to see my equipment? What's a Women's Community? Why do they hate you so much?"

Melian just kept walking. "It's a very long story, Boral."

"You could start," Boral said. "Nearly getting shot ought to be worth an explanation! Was any of that true?"

Melian glanced at him, the sweat running down his face. "A little of it. A little truth seasons a lie like salt does meat."

"Will you stop the parables and tell me what's going on?" Boral yelled.

"The Merrow believe in the strict separation of the sexes," Melian said. "After the age of three, males and females are not allowed to see each other except for arranged spouses, and that once every sixty-four Days. There are two kinds of settlements among the Merrow, and they do not mingle. Men live in Men's Communities and women in Women's Communities. We were indeed lucky to be found by a patrol from a Men's Community, because our presence would befoul women so much that we'd probably be shot."

"That's absurd," Boral said.

Melian shrugged. "It is their religious belief that complete separation of the sexes is the only way for either sex to be pure, just as they believe that the Third Lord is the only true god and that all other gods are manifestations of the Infernal."

"The Infernal?"

"The world." Melian gestured toward the rolling desert, the looming volcano beyond it. "The cruel world with its pain and suffering. We live in the Inferno, and the good are released from it into Paradise. And one day the sand will swallow up the sea, the mountains will darken the sky, and all souls will be released from the world." He shook his head tiredly. "I suppose I would say, if I were a scholar, that the Merrow religion resulted from the catastrophic volcanic eruption in the Lost Times, when the first human settlements on Menaechmi were destroyed and all knowledge of other worlds got lost for hundreds of years. That was more than a thousand years ago. I suppose for those who lived in those times it seemed that it truly was the end of the world."

"I think I read the first colony on Menaechmi was destroyed by a volcano," Boral said.

"It was. Not quite three hundred years after it was founded. The city was destroyed—all the infrastructure, the satellite links, the computer core. The solar panels were shattered by stones, the buildings destroyed by earthquake, and the ash lay as tall as we are over the ruins."

He stopped at the top of a dune to breathe. Boral got two water pouches out of his pack and handed him one. "Here," he said. "Got to stay hydrated."

"Many thanks," Melian said as he popped the seal. He took a deep drink. "But some survived. Some always do. There were farms and vineyards further out. And then the fishing fleet came in. They'd been out at sea and seen the eruption. They came in with full holds and took survivors up the coast to the farms that were in the other direction from the ash plume." He glanced at Boral. "The Golden Lady casts Her net, and some live and some die. But by Her favor, by the bounty of the sea, we lived and rebuilt."

"And the Merrow?" Boral asked.

Melian took another drink. "Their religion derives from those times, just as ours does. We both went in some strange directions." He gave Boral a sideways smile. "The Golden Lady's favor used to be bought with the blood of Her Husband. He still promises to give his life if it is called for. And for all our flaws, I cannot say that our rites are not beautiful."

"They are," Boral said. It wasn't like anything he'd ever imagined, but it was indeed beautiful. He took a drink. "What's this thing about you being a pervert?"

"I like women," he said. "I live with women. I sex women. I sleep with a woman in my bed. The Merrow way is very difficult for people who prefer the opposite sex. A man who sexes men can have his lover at his side his whole life, but a man who likes women is abominable. It's as hard on the women as the men, I think. Most women don't want to live in a Women's Community with no husbands, fathers or sons."

"No," Boral said. "I don't think many women want their sons taken away from them." He'd seen the mother of the youngest of the apprentices, Sai, when Master Castal-Edo had called her and let her see Sai onscreen for the first time in a year. She hadn't been able to stop crying the whole time she kept saying how happy she was.

Melian glanced at his manicured hands. "And there are no hapaloi. No hapaliae. No dissones. I couldn't live in their society. There would be no place for me." He shrugged. "And there is no place for many of them, which is why they want to leave."

"Why don't your people mingle?" Boral asked. "I mean, it seems like you would since you're just a few kilometers apart?"

Melian drank again. "They have sometimes, more than now. A hundred years ago there were Beiran mining operations in the desert not far from here. There were Merrow who came into Beira to trade. Some stayed. There were buildings in the city where they lived more or less according to their customs. Sometimes more, often less." He glanced sideways at Boral. "And you know what happens, don't you? Young people talk. Young people kiss. Young people marry. They have children who are neither or both." He took another drink. "And people hate. They hate those odd people, those strange ones. And some of the Merrow didn't disguise their disgust for Beirans and Beiran customs. They openly disrespected our gods. They said they weren't real or they were Infernal. They tried to convert people to their Covenant."

Boral nodded. "And the separation of the sexes wasn't possible."

"No, of course not. Our mining outposts employed people of all five genders. We refused to do otherwise. So Merrow saw males and females living together in their territory." He shook his head. "There was an incident at the mine. And then there was a riot in the city." He looked out over the dunes, toward the looming mountain. "I was five years old. We didn't live in the building we're in now. House Melian wasn't much in those days. The old building was smaller and closer to the sea. It had a honeybee carved beside the door—fancy I suppose, but I thought it was beautiful when I was a child. I rubbed its nose when I went in and out, for luck."

Boral took a drink. "What happened?" he asked quietly.

"The Merrow attacked the mine in force, taking back Merrow land. And then there was an anti-Merrow riot in the city. Someone launched an explosive through the second-floor windows." His voice was even, calm as a dreaming child. "I don't remember the explosion, just broken glass everywhere. My mother was killed. My father was critically injured. My grandmother…" He halted, then went on, still in that same even tone. "She thought my father would die. She feared I would be killed. She grabbed me and disappeared with me into the parts of the city she had lived in when she first came. The slums." He didn't look away from the distant mountain slopes. "I remember that. I remember hiding through the Full Day in a shattered building in clothes brown with someone's blood. I remember coming out at night to find water from a broken water main. I drank it out of my hands." Melian held out his hands, gold nails catching the light, turning them up and cupping the palms. "It can't have been more than two or three Days."

"That's terrible," Boral said.

Melian glanced at him, the corner of his mouth quirking. "Order was restored in the city. And then the Merrow counterattacked. They nearly reached the temple plaza, but not quite. Officially, House Melian's building was destroyed in the fighting. And then the Merrow were beaten back, street by street. You have no idea what urban warfare is like. Fifty thousand people died in the fighting, or from starvation or heat or lack of water. I wasn't one." Melian drained the water pouch. "My father was found in a medical center and he had a long convalescence but he lived. We were fully insured. We rebuilt."

Boral nodded. "And you promised it would never happen again."

For a moment Melian's face froze. "Yes," he said, looking away. "I suppose I did. I was five years old. I poured water through my fingers and promised that it would never happen again. Beira would never be destroyed again. We would not have this, not while I lived and breathed, not while I had strength to guard the city. We would have peace and nobody would be afraid again."

"And now you're the Guardian," Boral said.

"Yes." He took a deep breath. "I have spent fifty-one years building. Public water works, transient cubes so that no one is sleeping out in Full Day, port facilities that are the envy of the other Cities, temples and roads and parks and baths and shining towers full of cool apartments. And I will guard those things to my last breath." He looked at Boral. "War with Calpurnia could destroy it."

"It could," Boral said slowly, "But Guardian, I put it to you that you've done as much as you can to protect Beira with money. Now you have to protect it with ships. Sometimes you can't talk your way out of a jam. Sometimes you have to make alliances and fight."

"Now you sound like Aurore," he said. "My oldest daughter. She's eight or so years older than you."

"Maybe she's right," Boral said. "Morrigan can be a good friend, and it sounds like Menaechmi can use a good friend against the Calpurnians." He searched for the right words. "The Warlady wants alliances, and you're an honorable man."

"Goodness," Melian said, "nobody's ever accused me of honor before!"

"I think you'd keep your word," Boral said. "If it was to protect Beira."

"Yes." Melian took a deep breath. "Anything to protect Beira." He stowed the empty water pouch in his pack. "Since the war, we've had an impermeable border. We made a treaty with the Merrow. We do not go into their lands, and they do not come into ours. Our ways of life are simply incompatible. Contact results in conflict. The only way to avoid war is to avoid cultural contamination. That is their enormous problem with us, of course. Because their culture is so restrictive, ours seems very attractive by comparison to a lot of people. They don't let anyone consume our media or talk to us, and we help their Wise enforce it by agreeing that we will have no cultural contact." He shook his head. "And still there are runners. There are always Merrow who come out of the desert. Five years ago, when I became Guardian, I pushed through an asylum law."

"A what?" Boral said.

"That Merrow who came into Beiran territory would not be returned if they claimed asylum and said that they never intended to return and that they would assimilate to life in Beira. The asylum law wasn't popular in Beira, and the Merrow hate it. They believe, possibly rightly, that it encourages young people to run, so I am stealing their children." He shook his head. "But it's not in me to send people back to probable execution."

"No," Boral said slowly, "I couldn't do that either."

"It's not popular in Beira because once again there is an influx of Merrow. True, this time they must assimilate, but too many people remember what happened the last time we tried this." He gave Boral a sardonic smile. "Politics, young man. There are no easy answers and perhaps no right answers. We simply do what we think is least bad."

"And now maybe that's war with Calpurnia," Boral said.

"As much as I hate the idea," Melian said. He met Boral's eyes. "Tell your father I would welcome an envoy from Morrigan. I hope he will pass that on to the Warlady."

"I'll tell him," Boral promised.

CHAPTER THIRTEEN

Bister came back into the office after a quick run down the flightline. Every merchant ship had self-grounded due to the conflict above, and gossip was running rampant. It was useful to find out what it was. She knocked quietly, then opened the office door.

Caralys had a second screen moved in, a big one on a stand that was set to Beira Control. She was sitting at the desk, a small puddle of gold and pearls in her hands, her head down. She looked up, clear-eyed, and swallowed. "He left his jewelry here before he went on the Calpurnian ship." She turned a pearl and gold ring over in her hand. "He didn't expect to come back. That was his plan. He left a note."

Bister sat down in one of the chairs facing the desk. "Sometimes it's enough to offer the sacrifice," she said. "It doesn't have to be accepted." *Those long moments on Sounding Dark, alone with the Lady of the Void, waiting for impact with the Calpurnian ship....*

Caralys nodded. "He belongs to Her first. I know that. I understand what his oaths are." She put her head down on her hands over the jewelry. "There were things I needed to tell him, but I didn't think it was the right time. Give me a moment."

"Of course," Bister said.

Whatever else she would have said was interrupted by a comm chirp. "Gaura, we have an incoming call from the patrol. They have them!" Caralys closed her eyes. She didn't look like she could say something right this moment.

Bister toggled the mic open. "Both of them?"

"The Guardian and the young xalepos, yes. They're both in good medical condition. They're giving an ETA in thirty-four minutes. They're near Seismic Seven on the Old Man."

"Wonderful," Caralys said. She had found her voice. "Many thanks." She switched the channel, glancing at Bister. "I'm calling House Melian. Nariah? This is Caralys. Can you give me Phoebe, please." She waited a moment. "Phoebe? It's Cara. He's been found and he's all right. So you and Theo know…."

Bister got up and went out into the main control room. Caralys might appreciate a few minutes of privacy. She'd thought Boral was a good bet, and it had turned out she was right. Bister looked out over the empty launch pads, the concrete white in the sun. It looked like a regular day on Inanna, one sun in the sky. No ships were being towed out and no launches marred the perfect sky. The last thing a merchanter wanted was to boost into the middle of a battle. But was there going to be a battle?

Lady, Bister thought, *much as I appreciate the occasional cryptic hint, is there any chance I could get a shove? Right now we're at a stalemate.* She closed her eyes. *It would be great if the Altissimi would just jump out of here. Why don't they?*

I am not the one who pursues them. It was like a quiet voice, like her own voice in her head. *Pride brings the high down when they forget whom they serve, and the Hounds pursue oathbreakers.*

Bister waited, but there was nothing more. "Great, that's so helpful," Bister said aloud. Being the avatar of the Lady of the Void had been completely unexpected—an accident, Bister thought sometimes. At the very least, any training or information she was supposed to receive had been curtailed. Whatever it was she was supposed to know, whatever sanctity might have been supposed to descend on her, remained a mystery. She was still Bister, only with this little whisper in her head sometimes.

Boral, the Morriganian electromancer, had called her a Dreamer. Bister frowned, looking out at the empty tarmac. As far as she knew, Dreamers were the priestly caste on Morrigan. She'd never met one on all the times she'd been to Morrigan. Why would she? They were rare and high-ranking. Her trips to Morrigan had involved reasonably priced establishments around the starport and some shopping to pick up things that Inanna needed. She'd seen the Sema from a distance, but she'd certainly never been inside. It was a temple to a Morriganian god—a deified man, the Warlord. Some folks like Perisad had a little shrine the size of a storefront to him on the Glitter Rim in Eresh, but that was the limit of her familiarity. He was a god for warriors. Bister wasn't that. She was a fixer, a smuggler, a sometime thief. A Dreamer? What was a Dreamer anyway?

Bister shook her head. Maybe the answer to that was on Morrigan. Certainly there were other reasons to go there. But first this situation had to resolve. If Tal went after the Calpurnian ship, it had the speed to come around the planet faster, keeping Menaechmi between them. No, his best bet was to back off to a distance where he could get a plot, but that would be far enough to leave Beira mostly unprotected. Why didn't they just jump out? Had Tal damaged their main engines with his good shot? Or was it simply pride? Was that what the Lady of the Void had hinted? Cassian could run, but he wouldn't? Sooner or later he had to either attack or run. He couldn't just sit there forever. It would make him look weak and indecisive. No, she'd seen men like him her whole life. He'd attack.

A trundle was pulling up beside the building, a brown one with some kind of symbol on the side, its caterpillar treads dirty. The doors winged open, two figures getting out. The reporters made a rush, nearly knocking the passengers back inside before somebody started organizing them. The nearer one was a tall young man with dark skin and a confident air.

Well, Bister thought, *Boral's learned a thing or two*. She ambled over toward the trundle. The reporters were mobbing Helios Melian, who looked sunburned and was wearing a sweat-soaked blue shirt rather than finery. Boral was backing slowly away unheeded. "Holla, Boral," Bister said.

He jumped, then saw who it was. "Bister. Am I glad to see you! It's been a wild—I don't know. How long has it been?"

"You know I can never keep track of time on this crazy planet," Bister said. "Come on in and get cool and have some of whatever meal it is they've sent out for before this madhouse follows." She nodded with her chin toward Helios Melian and the haggle of reporters.

"He's not so bad," Boral said. "I see why he has the Golden Lady's favor."

Bister's eyebrows rose. "Sounds like you've had a heart-to-heart."

"Kinda." Boral followed her into the front of the control center and accepted a cold pouch of juice gratefully. "I need to get back to my ship."

"That's hard to do because they're in high orbit," Bister said.

"What?" Boral nearly spat juice everywhere. "They left me?"

"They launched when the shooting started. They're hanging around in high orbit watching."

Boral nodded. "The Old Man is probably petrified of going back and telling the Warlady that he misplaced his electromancer. But we're not supposed to get into a fight with the Calpurnians."

"Your scoutship is outgunned about five to one," Bister observed. "So, no."

Helios Melian had come inside, two or three staff clearing a way into the building with a cheer. He greeted Praxi warmly, the disson attempting to pry him away from the reporters, no doubt with a report on what was happening. The other staff stopped the reporters who shouted questions at the lobby doors.

"Oh, I've got his tunic," Boral said, pulling the pack off his back. "I bet he wants that." He made his way across the control center, followed by Bister.

Caralys was standing in the office doorway, shaking her head with a smile on her face as Melian glad-handed his way to her. He gave the crowd a smile, then walked up to her and took her in a passionate kiss, her arms going around him and his hand on the back of her head. The room full of staff cheered.

Bister laughed. "It's a statement," she said. "Helios Melian is back."

"He's lucky to be standing on his feet," Boral said quietly. "The desert was rough. He needs water and cool more than I do."

"Never let them see you down," Bister said. She understood that completely.

Melian and Caralys went in the office, Praxi following. They closed the door and opaqued it. Bister and Boral followed, Boral knocking. "It's me. Boral. Can I come in?"

Caralys opened the door. "Yes. And Bister."

Melian was sitting at the desk looking considerably less perky than he had a few minutes before. "I have your tunic," Boral said, opening his pack and pulling out the embroidered fabric. "I thought you'd need that."

"To look half-decent, yes." Melian reached up to take it. "Thank you, Boral."

"Boral, could you go get him some water and something light to eat?" Caralys asked. "I've had food brought in for the staff and it's set up in the main room."

"Sure," Boral said as Melian put his arm in one sleeve, wincing.

"What's wrong?" Caralys asked.

"Sunburned arms." Melian shoved his arms in, pulling the tunic tight and buttoning the top button. "But that's the least of our worries."

"Let me," Caralys said, attending to the rest of the tiny buttons. She just wanted to touch him, Bister thought, and well enough. He slid the pearl and gold ring onto his finger.

Praxi was looking at Beira Control's plot, switching back and forth between satellite views. "It looks like the Calpurnians are firing steering thrusters," they said.

"Are we under a full weather lockdown?" Melian asked Caralys. "Everyone to storm shelters?"

"I don't have the authority to order that," Caralys said. "And neither does Arsenio. I sent House Melian into the storm shelter."

"Then get me an emergency line to the Advisory," Melian said. "We're doing it. It's the safest thing if the Calpurnians fire on the city."

"You know the shelters will hold less than half the population," Praxi said.

"Yes, I know that," Melian snapped. "And generally with a tropical cyclone we have days of warning to evacuate. But less than half the population is better than none."

"The line is active," Caralys said, and Melian leaned into the pickup.

Bister wandered over by the door, looking at the screen with the satellite plot. The Calpurnian was definitely maneuvering. Maybe they'd made repairs and were testing them? Boral came back with more water and two flatbread rolls and Bister let him in. "What's going on?" he asked as he put them on the table near Melian.

Bister shrugged. "The Calpurnians are testing their thrusters, I think. *Ivory Three* and *Spider* are both holding station."

There was a sudden shrill shrieking, the weather alert alarms sounding, echoing through the building from several sirens. Boral jumped. "What's that?"

"Weather alert," Bister said. "To tell people to get to shelters."

"Call coming in from *Ivory Three*," Praxi said.

"Put them on," Melian said.

Tal's voice was crystal clear. "*Liberty* is maneuvering. We're moving to intercept them away from Beira as soon as we see their trajectory." Melian looked at Caralys, his mouth quirking as if to say, *The pirates are your call,* Bister thought.

Caralys leaned toward the mic. "Many thanks, Ivory Captain."

Boral nudged Bister. "Where's *Spider*?"

"Up there," Bister said. "In the upper left corner of the screen."

"What is the Captain doing?" Boral wondered aloud.

A tech in Melian colors stuck his head in the door. "Your pardon, Guardian, but the nets need a statement. The Advisory just sent a weather evac code and people are panicking."

"I'm coming." Melian got to his feet, straightening the collar of his elaborate tunic. "I'll give them all the same live feed from directly in front of the building on the flight line. No need for the haggle of reporters in here." He glanced at Caralys. "You have this?"

"Yes," she said. She switched half the split screen to a different satellite view. "Ivory Captain, we see what suggests a great circle loop over the southern pole and coming up over the ocean to our west."

"Thanks, Beira Control," Tal said easily. "Felony, put us on a course to intercept over the ocean. Hold at four hundred kilometer altitude."

"Changing course, captain," someone said behind him. On the screen, *Ivory* slowly began to come about.

Very slowly, Bister thought. She'd gotten used to *Steel Nine* when she was aboard ships from Eresh, larger but much newer and more maneuverable. *Ivory* moved like a leviathan in a gravity well, which would explain why Tal was holding off so far. If he lost too much altitude, the burn to regain it would render them vulnerable. He didn't dare dip into the ionosphere.

The Calpurnian was moving faster. It was indeed coming in on a great circle route over the south pole, then coming into Beira and the Cities of the Coast obliquely from the southwest. The altitude was reading three hundred kilometers, satellite level. They'd taken the measure of *Ivory*, Bister thought. Tal would have to come to them if he wanted to close.

Tal didn't seem perturbed. "Clear the forward tube for a 750," he said. "Murder, get me a plot the moment you have one."

On the screen, the two ships were closing in three dimensions, thousands of miles between them still, but now on a direct course for each other over the western sea. Caralys looked up at Bister, the mic off. "Can he do it?"

"They're well-matched," Bister said. "*Ivory* has heavier armament, but *Liberty* is more maneuverable. It's close."

"Understood," Caralys said. She fidgeted with something on the desk as she watched the plot, Helios's gold and pearl earrings that he hadn't put back on yet.

The range closed quickly. They were both moving very fast. The curvature of the world was modeled in three dimensions, *Ivory*'s altitude giving it an advantage. "Fire when you bear," Tal said. A second later the 750 streaked away. "Reload the tube with another 750," Tal said. "Two 500s in the ventral tubes, please."

"He's hitting them as hard as he can right off," Bister said to Caralys. "That's a lot of ordnance." Boral crowded in behind her to watch.

Caralys held her breath. "How many does he carry?"

"Probably four to eight 750s and ten or twelve 500s," Bister said. "He's already given them a pair of 500s, so ten maybe." Which ought to be a gracious plenty to utterly destroy *Liberty*. Ought to be.

"Fire the 500s," Tal said.

Behind him, someone said, "Captain, the 750 has acquired."

"Load countermeasures packets in the ventral tubes," Tal said.

"What's that for?" Caralys asked Bister.

"That," Bister pointed. "*Liberty* just fired a pair of 500s too."

The two ships continued on course for each other, closing at fifteen hundred kilometers per hour. At this rate they'd pass one hundred kilometers apart, *Ivory*'s belly to *Liberty*'s back if neither captain flinched. The 750 wavered on the plot and then disappeared. "Argh," Bister said. "It hit the countermeasures."

"Launch our countermeasures," Tal said. He was leaning forward in his seat now, the straps over his shoulders straining. "Hold the 750 in the tube. We'll give it to them when we pass. Less time for countermeasures."

Bister shook her head. If she were Cassian, she wouldn't try a close pass with a ship that launched 750s. What was the plan here? And then it was clear. "Tal," she said, opening the comm, "once they're past you, they've got an open run for Beira. You can't turn fast enough. He's not trying to beat you. He's trying to make an example of Beira for the other Cities of the Coast."

One of *Liberty*'s 500s hit *Ivory*'s countermeasures, wavering and dropping toward the sea. Boral had his fists clenched. All this was happening hundreds of kilometers out at sea. "Two more live missiles running," Boral said. "One from each."

Bister gritted her teeth. The range was closing. A 500 slammed into *Liberty*'s nose, the explosion rocking the entire ship. Even now sirens must be wailing decompression, compartments sealing against vacuum, and still *Liberty* came on.

"Evasive!" Tal shouted. "Take us down to three hundred!"

Too late, Bister thought. *Liberty*'s 500 plowed a line of fire along *Ivory*'s spine, taking out the dorsal missile launchers. Not much structural damage, and the atmosphere plume was small, but the loss of the launchers meant that their ordnance was now equal.

Alarms hooted in *Ivory*'s command center as they tried to dive, a tighter pass between them. "Fire the 750!" Tal said.

It streaked across the sky, diving toward *Liberty*. Almost simultaneously *Liberty* fired. "Shit," Bister said. It wasn't the dorsal launcher at *Ivory*, but a 500 running from the ventral launcher straight ahead, toward Beira now not five hundred kilometers away. There was nothing between the missile and Beira except sky and sea.

Ivory was trying to turn, dropping down as it banked, sliding to an altitude below three hundred kilometers. Two hundred fifty. Two hundred. Atmospheric drag slowed it further. Caralys caught her breath.

"Look!" Boral said. A wedge moved on the plot, the scoutship *Spider* dropping like a kestrel in a dive toward the sea right in front of the missile. "It's acquired on *Spider*!"

Spider was running flat out toward the coast, the missile just behind. Bister saw it go to a full burn, nose turning up, the missile turning with it.

"Come on! Come on!" Boral shouted. It shouldn't be able to outrun a missile, but it could stay even, an all-engine burn as the little scoutship shot up on full thrusters. "Come on, Paloma! Give it the juice!"

Spider shot upward, leaving the atmosphere completely, the missile in pursuit. But a 500 had a limited amount of solid fuel. Once it was burned out, the missile was purely ballistic. Already it sputtered, following *Spider* around the curve of the planet. *Spider* was making the missile spend fuel to adjust course. It flamed out, slipping sideways as the gravity well claimed it, beginning a slow, harmless fall toward the distant ocean.

Meanwhile, *Ivory* clawed for the turn, trying to come about at only fifty kilometers. *Liberty* had dropped low as well, lining up the perfect shot. From its cameras, the coast must be rising out of the sea, Beira's towers shining in the bright sun.

"I think we should go down to the basement," Bister said quietly as Melian came back in.

He looked at her sharply. "We're in the storm surge zone. The port offices don't have basements."

Liberty fired. *Ivory* fired at the same moment, but they were way back, still far out to sea. Caralys stood up. *Liberty*'s 500 streaked toward Beira. "There is nowhere to go," she said. She looked toward the window, toward the sea. The contrail was clearly visible, the missile approaching faster than the speed of sound.

"Shit," Bister said as Boral pushed past her. *Ivory* had a missile running, but it wouldn't do them much good. There was no way *Spider* could get there in time either. "Six seconds to impact."

Melian reached for Caralys's hand and she reached for his, both of them looking straight out to sea. Boral threw his hand up, legs braced as though he intended to lift the world. His eyes closed, his face taut with strain.

"Five seconds," Bister said. "Four. Three. Two." The missile turned. It looped up, turning back on the course of its own contrail. Boral fell to his knees.

"It's acquired on *Liberty*!" Bister said. Every alarm on *Liberty* must be sounding. It was sandwiched between two running missiles, the one *Ivory* had launched and its own. Its own hit first, plowing into the already damaged nose, exploding deep in *Liberty*'s vitals, secondary explosions incandescing even in bright sunlight. *Ivory*'s missile hit a second later, striking just forward of the main engines. *Liberty* broke in half. A rain of material and people began a long fall to the sea.

Bister ran to Boral's side, getting her shoulder beneath his. His eyes were defocused. "I got it," he said. "I got the guidance."

"Yes," Bister said. "You did." She'd never imagined anything like that, the power to turn a missile with sheer will. No wonder Morrigan kept its electromancers close and shrouded in secrecy.

"Is it over?" Boral asked.

Bister looked at the fireball out to sea. "Yes," she said.

Chapter Fourteen

Boral and Bister were sitting in hard plastic seats in a corner of the control room while everyone ran around doing things. No one was paying any attention to them. Boral was eating some kind of pastry with cream in the middle. It was really good.

Helios Melian approached. He definitely looked like he was feeling much better. "I haven't thanked you," Melian said.

Boral stood up. He still had the pastry in his hand, so he turned and put it down. "It's fine. Really. I mean…."

"You saved my life and my city," Melian said. He looked tired and sunburned but basically all right, which Boral was glad of. "I am in your debt."

"About that," Boral said. "Nobody can know." Melian raised an eyebrow and he continued. "Nobody is supposed to know exactly what electromancers can do. We're a state secret. That's why we haven't been allowed off the ship even when we served in wartime, except in a Morriganian port. The new rules just went into effect and I blew them up." Boral searched for the words. "So it has to stay a secret. Nobody can know that an electromancer was anywhere around."

"And how am I supposed to explain what happened to the missile?" Melian asked. "Hundreds of people saw it turn around. Everyone here, everyone at Beira Control, all the monitoring stations, not to mention eyewitnesses. I have all the nets in the lobby waiting for an explanation."

"I can answer that," Bister said, standing up. "I'm the operative you hired to rescue the crew of *Light Dancer*. When I was aboard the Calpurnian ship I sabotaged some of the missiles that it carried. Fortunately, that was one of them. I'm an expert operative. Good thing I was hired by Helios Melian."

'You sabotaged the missile to acquire on the ship that fired it?" Melian said skeptically.

"Like I said, I'm an expert operative," Bister said with a cocky grin.

"Not an electromancer," Boral said. "Just a good saboteur."

Melian nodded thoughtfully. "That could work. And you, Boral. Your scoutship is landing. Praxi tells me your captain wants you to come aboard urgently."

"Yeah, I bet." Boral winced. The Old Man was going to have a lot to say. He had some explaining to do, and most likely a quick trip back to Morrigan. But the Warlady couldn't be too angry, right? He'd saved a city and made a potential ally. Surely that was all good. His father would have a fit, but it would mostly be because he would have been worried if he'd known. But he'd told him to have experiences, and Boral certainly had.

He didn't expect it when Melian embraced him, a good solid hug like his father would give him. "You are always welcome in Beira," he said.

"Thank you," Boral said. "And I mean it." Something had changed in him. Only time would show him what it was. He let go. "What about Bister?"

Melian turned to Bister with a smile. "I believe Cara promised you equipment for Inanna," he said. "And a complete repudiation of the Isolation." He handed her his screen. "The Husband of the Golden Lady, speaking for Her and Her temple, hereby repudiates the Treaty of Isolation enforced on Inanna as inhumane and unnecessary, a historical artifact of its time that no longer holds force. Additionally, the Guardian of Beira offers his thanks to Bister of Inanna for her services to the city. In light of our appreciation, Inanna is granted free and open trade rights to the City of Beira."

"That's really positive," Boral said. "You can do it just like that?"

Melian smiled. "Today I can. Tomorrow it will be yesterday's news. But this will go out on the nets today and there's a formal copy for you. So shall we go explain to the press how this is a small token of our thanks to the saboteur whose clever reprogramming of missiles saved the city?"

"That sounds fabulous," Bister said, breaking into a wide smile as Melian offered her his arm. "If I'd known I was going on camera, I'd have worn my clean shirt."

"I expect somebody can find you one," Helios Melian said as he escorted her away.

He'd better get back to the ship before someone came looking for him, Boral thought.

"Where in the name of Blessed Khreesos have you been?" the Old Man demanded, his hands on his hips.

"It's complicated, Captain," Boral said, standing very straight.

"Get your ass on this ship right this minute," the Captain said. "Over-lieutenant, ask Beira Control for immediate departure clearance. We're getting out of here before anything else happens."

"Yes, Captain," Paloma said, giving Boral a warning look and heading for the control center.

"I don't even know what to say," the Captain said. He looked harried. "Except when you see a missile make a U-turn, you know it's your missing electromancer."

"I can explain," Boral began.

"You can explain in the gaps between jumps," the Captain said.

"We've got three jumps to Morrigan, and if the Warlady doesn't have my command I'll be shocked."

"Not when she hears that the Guardian of Beira wants to talk about an alliance against Calpurnia," Boral said. "She'll be really glad to hear that. And we did save the city. Both of us. Because that missile interception was just plain brilliant!"

The Captain looked abashed. "What was I going to do? Let some Calpurnian bastard blow up a city?"

"My point exactly," Boral said. "So we just explain. And give her Helios Melian's message that he would welcome an official emissary from the Warlady. We ace diplomacy."

"Right." The Captain shook his head.

Paloma called on the inboard. "Captain, we are cleared for immediate departure."

"Go strap yourself in," the Captain said. "We'll talk later."

Boral followed him to the cramped command center, sliding into his couch, reclining it, and carefully buckling all the straps while the main engines came online. The scoutship tilted ninety degrees into the launch position to the familiar sounds of the launch cradle as it locked.

"Engage main thrusters," the Captain said, and the Morriganian scoutship *Spider* rose on a column of fire.

The camera angled down, the screen showing Beira and its coast, the city becoming indistinct as they slipped through a thin cloud layer, then up into the bright sun. *Ivory Three* rode in low orbit, spacers in suits out on the dorsal surface making repairs. Boral resisted the urge to wave. Of course they couldn't see him. Menaechmi curved beneath him gold and blue, desert and sea, and the fragile, glittering strip between. *Gold and blue to black and gray, and dark to wash the stars away....* It was part of some poem his father had recited, and it must be about a takeoff like this.

I'll be back, Boral promised silently. *And I'll go lots of other places too.*

It had been a good day.

It was Full Day before it was possible to leave the port office. The large House Melian trundle picked them up, and Caralys climbed into its plush interior gratefully. Bister got in with them, sitting on the backward facing seat. Her clothes and other things were still at House Melian, and she had agreed to be their guest until *Ivory Three* was relieved by a second Name Ship in the coming weeks, an additional deterrent to any further incursions from Calpurnia. It would be expensive paying privateers to guard Beira, but it was a necessary expense.

Which was another problem, of course, Caralys thought. Helios would need to find out anything his agents on Calpurnia could discover. What faction ruled now? Who was on top? What did they want? But those were problems for another day. This day had been long enough already.

Helios nearly fell asleep on the short ride back to the House, his head back against the Melian Blue seat rest. He stirred as they parked. "I need to see Theo and Mia first," he said. "To make sure Theo is all right and let Mia know I am too."

"Of course," Caralys said as they waited for the lift. "And then rest."

Caralys thought that Bister didn't seem at all reluctant to sample House Melian's luxury and made a mental note to make sure that she was comfortable and enjoyed her stay as their guest. She owed Bister more than she could possibly repay. She saw Bister to a lavish guest suite and left her at the door, Bister heading for the sleeping closet, and then continued down the hall.

Caralys opened the door to the bath. It was quiet, the pool serene and silent, ripples spreading on its surface. No one at all was there, the heat of Full Day being a usual sleeping time. Aurore and Dian would be home soon. Aurore had been right about arming the merchant vessels; Helios would do it now, and that was more currency, but it had to be.

Gratefully, Caralys took off the high-fashion dress she'd put on to attend the rite forty hours earlier. It looked as much the worse for wear as she felt. She ducked under a swift spray, feeling as though she were rinsing off a thousand years of worry. A proper bath could wait.

She put on a gauze robe and padded down the empty hall, through the anteroom and study, into Helios's sleeping closet. It was quiet and dark, black linen and thick carpet, walls painted midnight blue, the sleep-light of blue glass hanging from the ceiling. The net pattern in gold on the glass reflected against the walls, as though she were underwater in a net of light. And it was still there, not blown up by a Calpurnian missile. Which was more than she'd expected at one point.

Helios wasn't there. Of course. He'd gone to see Theo and Mia. No one would know if she simply waited for him just a few minutes.

Caralys woke when Helios sat down on the side of the bed. His hair was wet; he must have stopped at the bath too, and he was slathering herbal cream on his arms. "Can you get the back of my neck?" he asked.

Caralys sat up, letting the covers fall away and angling behind him. She took the pouch of cream. He looked better, but it had certainly been a long forty-nine hours since he left for the bull-slaying. Now that he was naked, she could see the lines of his tunic on his skin at the neck and arms, but sunburn would heal quickly. She squeezed the cream into her palm and started applying it. Helios sighed.

"Do you remember," she said to the back of his neck, "that years ago you told me that ambition comes on later in life, and asked me what I would want if I could have nearly anything?"

"Yes," he said. "What is it you want?" He turned to see her face.

"I want to be Guardian of Beira," Caralys said.

His eyes were warm, and there was that little smile that tugged at the right corner of his mouth. "I think you will make a fine Guardian of Beira," he said.

"In time," she said. "Not anytime soon."

"No, not anytime soon." He turned around, gathering her in, and she rested her head against his shoulder, trying to avoid the parts sticky with sun cream. Not anytime soon, not now, but he was twenty-six years her senior. There would be a time.

"I've been thinking too," he said from somewhere above her left ear. "Your contract is up soon. I'd like to offer you a more favorable one. Full House membership, a generous financial package including interest in two or three House Melian merchant vessels, and the stipulation that you never have to obey me in anything."

Caralys laughed. "I'm not sure 'never have to obey you' is a good legal clause. Maybe we should elaborate on just where and when you are the master." She lifted her head to meet his lips, sweet and passionate and so hungry.

"If that suits you," he said, when they broke apart. "Those clauses will be worth three Days' story when they leak to the gossip columns."

"I expect so," Caralys said.

"I was thinking a four-year contract."

"Four years?"

He shrugged as he always did when he had something to say that mattered. "In four years I'll be sixty. It will be time to step down from the Golden Lady's service. It's better to walk away than to fail."

"Helios Melian never fails," Caralys said gently. "But yes, there's a time."

"I will cease being Her Husband," Helios said. "So if your contract is up again shortly thereafter…." He stopped, his eyes on hers, watching her expression. "It can't hurt your ambition to be

Guardian of Beira someday to be Helios Melian's widow."

Caralys looked at him. "That is the worst offer of a marriage contract I've ever heard," she said.

"How many have you heard?" His mouth twitched.

She pulled him down to her. "I don't want to even think about that. I nearly lost you today. I'm not going to imagine the day that I do."

"Then think about the arrangements before then," he said, settling beside her, one hand making lazy circles on her thigh. "A contract with full House membership and the freedom to do whatever you want. And then...."

"I would rather be your wife than your widow," she said. She kissed him again, pulling him tight against her and arranging the linens so that they snuggled in the cool, black sheets.

"That generally does come first."

She put her hand to the side of his face. "You know I love you with all my heart."

"And I you, my Cara. Whatever heart I have."

"My dear, you wear it on your sleeve," she said. He might lie about what he knew or what he intended, but his feelings were always perfectly plain. She was the one with the gambler's face. She had bet her heart and lost it, gaining his in the process. Another kiss, slow and warm. She eventually came up. "I thought you wanted Aurore to follow in your footsteps."

Helios sighed, plopping back against the pillows. "Aurore wants to play soldier. When she gets home, I will have to tell her that she was right about arming the merchant ships, and then we will see what happens. She has no interest in the government of Beira. She'll be head of House Melian, but you would be a better Guardian. And keep it all in the family." He smirked. "No one will ever be rid of me."

Caralys laughed. She propped up on one elbow so that she could see his face. It was time. "Helios, I'm fourteen Days pregnant."

His expression was wonderful to see, first delight and surprise, then utter smugness as he pulled her down for a kiss. "Caralys. Precious Cara."

"I wanted to wait until I knew it was all right," she said, and to her surprise her voice shook. "Until the genetic tests were good— and then Theo was kidnapped and there was the rite and you were missing and…" Another long kiss interrupted this litany. She settled on his shoulder. "How would you like another little girl?"

"Another little girl would be perfect," he said, stroking her damp hair. "I am the luckiest man that ever lived."

"You have fortune's favor," she said, and closed her eyes against him in the sleeping closet, caught in the faint golden net of light.

Appendix: The Gods of Space

The beliefs of the peoples of the eight of the known Nine Worlds are complex, as one might expect of a society of billions of people more than two thousand years removed from a common origin. Philosophies and social ideologies abound. However, in the last centuries since contact was reestablished between eight of the nine worlds, seven of them have come to share a common pantheon of gods, though various deities are emphasized more in some places than in others, and even the same god may have different aspects and attributes on different worlds. These are the Lady of the Void, the Lord of the Dance, the Golden Lady, Mother Death, the Hunter, the Artifex, and the Warlord. There are others who are worshipped more locally beyond these main ones.

The Lady of the Void is the oldest of the pantheon, first called upon by the voyagers from distant Earth who ventured into the long night beyond heliopause. She is the Void itself, vast and timeless, beginning and ending, generally portrayed as a woman in a gown of stars holding the accretion disk of a black hole in one hand and a newborn star in the other. She is the goddess of voyagers. Those who die in space are remanded to her, and it is said that she takes the blood of those lost in the void as her offering; even today libations are poured to her in wine with the maiden voyage of a new ship or a particularly hazardous journey undertaken. And yet she is also called upon as Mother of Mercy, interceding for her human children and loving them deeply. In ancient times, her priests were literal Navigators, those who guided the great generation ships that led people to the Nine Worlds. Today, most of her worshippers are star voyagers and her devotions are a minority practice everywhere.

The Lord of the Dance is her lover, god of green and growing things, He Who Brings the Rains. He calls to her from fertile worlds, drawing her out of the long night to join him in love in some beautiful place, before she returns to the stars like a comet on a long orbit. He is a fertility god and a god of vegetation, generally seen as benign and worshipped with dance and song. However, he has a Dark Face, the psychopomp who goes between the living and the dead, who passes through the doors of night without harm and whose Hounds pursue criminals to the ends of the universe.

Once, he was one of the principal gods of Calpurnia, Menaechmi and Lono, though different aspects were emphasized. Lono saw him as dual, Light Face and Dark Face, while on Menaechmi the Light Face predominated, with the Dark Face remaining a mystery for initiates, his requirements hidden. Calpurnia has more or less relegated the Lord of the Dance to "folkloric heritage." While there are still historic temples there, they are museums; and actual worship is frowned upon as plebeian and ignorant. Those who see him as more than metaphor generally don't talk about it. Menaechmi and Lono both have active temples and priesthoods, notably the Theon at Ancyra on Menaechmi and the Shrine at Tranquility on Lono.

The Golden Lady is the daughter of the union of the Lady of the Void and the Lord of the Dance. This can certainly be read as metaphor—commerce, prosperity, trade and fortune derive from agricultural abundance and the mastery of the starlanes. She is usually pictured as a beautiful woman in a golden gown with a vessel that pours out bounty. She is worshipped throughout the worlds, but her principal temple is in the city of Beira on Menaechmi. It is there that she takes a mortal man as Husband who reigns with her a year and then undergoes ritual death. This is perhaps a vestige of human sacrifice in the Dark Years when star travel was lost, though in modern times the death is purely symbolic and the Husband a priest who serves a number of years and then retires. As patron of commerce, many merchant starships invoke her in their name, such as *Golden Promise*.

Mother Death, also known as the Scorpion Queen, is one of the more enigmatic members of the pantheon. Perhaps she was originally the deity of uninhabitable places or environments marginal for human life. She rules over aridity, cold, heat, and barrenness. She is sole, unrelated to the others, rather than part of a family grouping. She is also the guardian of honor, and there are stories in which the Lord of the Dance in his Dark Face visits her or is trapped by her or courts her and escapes her. Many worlds had isolated shrines to her, but her worship has always been ascetic and removed from civic life. Those who seek her renounce the world, and yet she is always there on the edge of stories, a mystery at the verge.

The Hunter is the son of the Lord of the Dance, born of his union with a water spirit, and is portrayed as a bold young man with a spear, either mounted on or in the process of slaying a great sea leviathan. One tale from Inanna tells that he was called upon by the frantic family of a princess who had been taken by a leviathan, and he rescued her from the deeps and married her beneath a full moon, father to a royal line. The same tale is told on Lono with a few changes as the origin story of the line of Calado princes, though which story came first is unknown. He is the quintessential young hero, brave and trustworthy and incorruptible.

The Artifex, also known as the Lady of Fires on Inanna, was a woman who became a smith or artificer or engineer depending on where the story is told. She was so the master of her element that she built a new body for herself or modified her body to become the Artifex, nonbinary and imperishable, immortal and perfected.

They are the god of art and science, of things built and made by human hands, transformed and transforming. Through their art, ore becomes iron and sand becomes glass. Through their science, illness is cured, the blind see, and crushed limbs are replaced with ones of silicone and steel. Through their genius, ships fold space and worlds are terraformed, satellites circling in belts of light. The Artifex is the official god of the Adelpha Rim; and though they are worshipped throughout the worlds, they are less popular on Calpurnia and Lono than elsewhere. Some have theorized that the Aritfex's original story is based on a real person from the Dark Years, but that is supposition.

The Warlord is the youngest of the pantheon and is certainly based upon a real person. Khreesos was the leader who unified Morrigan eight hundred years ago, as the Dark Years ended with the invention of the jump drive. He had a spectacular twenty-year career in which he built an empire that included six of the nine worlds before his death at forty-five, while attempting to find the missing world of Amurru. His consciousness was transferred into the computer core of his ship and hence to the Core on Morrigan, which then became known as the Presence. Since then, the Warlord has guided Morrigan as titular deity. He is the god of strategy and war. His worship has slowly spread off Morrigan, though more than the others he is still perceived as the god of a people.

While there are other deities worshipped in minority populations, such as the Third Lord of the Merrow of Menaechmi, they are distinctly local. As contact between the worlds has intensified, this common worship holds them together like the Golden Lady's net.

Acknowledgments

The author would like to extend her thanks to those who kindly read and commented on *Fortune's Favor* before its publication: Victoria Francis, Melissa Scott, Lena Strid, and my wonderful partner, Amy Griswold. I would also like to thank my editor, Athena Andreadis, who has improved *Fortune's Favor* immeasurably with her editorial suggestions.

About the Author

Jo Graham is the author of twenty-seven books and three online games. Best known for her historical fantasy novels *Black Ships* and *Stealing Fire*, and her tie-in novels for MGM's popular *Stargate: Atlantis* and *Stargate: SG-1* series, she has been a Locus Award finalist, an Amazon Top Choice, a Spectrum Award finalist, a Romantic Times Top Pick in historical fiction and a Lambda Literary Award and Rainbow Award nominee for bisexual fiction. With Melissa Scott, she is the author of five books in the *Order of the Air* series, a historical fantasy series set in the 1920s and 30s. She is also the author of three pagan spirituality books. She lives in North Carolina with her partner and is the mother of two daughters.